To Deborah, Alexander and Clementine
With thanks for your comment and criticism and,
above all, your forbearance.

THE MAIN CHARACTERS

The Romans
Festus Marcus Maximus, a centurion in the Jerusalem garrison
Cornelius Marcus Lucius, a junior officer in the Jerusalem garrison
Pontius Pilate, the Governor of Judea
Claudia Procula, the wife of Pontius Pilate

The Jewish leaders
Joseph, son of Caiaphas, also called Caiaphas, the High Priest
Annas, son of Seth, Joseph's father-in-law and a former High Priest
Jonathan, the Captain of the Temple Guards
Eleazar, a lawyer
Reuben, Eleazar's assistant
Nicodemus, a member of the Sanhedrin, the Jewish council
Barrabas, a guerrilla leader

The Galileans
Jeshua, son of Joseph, a prophet from Nazareth
Judah, also called Iscariot, a disciple and treasurer of Jeshua's travelling band
Gad, a merchant from Tiberias in Galilee
Amos, Gad's brother and business partner
Anna, Gad's wife
Benjamin, Gad and Anna's son

Jerusalem cAD30

JOHN BRIDGES

THE
BLOOD
OF
INNOCENTS

Matador
9 Priory Business Park,
Wistow Road, Kibworth Beauchamp,
Leicestershire. LE8 0RX
Tel: (+44) 116 279 2299
Fax: (+44) 116 279 2277
Email: books@troubador.co.uk
Web: www.troubador.co.uk/matador

ISBN 978 1780881 225

British Library Cataloguing in Publication Data.
A catalogue record for this book is available from the British Library.

Typeset in 11pt Aldine401 BT Roman by Troubador Publishing Ltd, Leicester, UK

Matador is an imprint of Troubador Publishing Ltd

Printed and bound in the UK by TJ International, Padstow, Cornwall

PART ONE

THREE WEEKS BEFORE PASSOVER

CHAPTER 1

Judean desert, west of the Dead Sea, Sunday afternoon

Centurion Festus Marcus Maximus had seen more suffering than he could remember. This youngster though, had been screaming for so long now that even Maximus was finding it tiresome. Blood still spattered onto the rocks from the boy's leg where a spear had torn into his thigh, ending his attempt to escape.

The Samaritan auxiliaries under his command quietly hated Hebrew rebels. Maximus guessed that meant the weapon was probably torn out of his leg as roughly as possible. His men may have hoped that shock and blood loss would mean no wounded prisoner to carry back to Jerusalem. Some muscle below his hip seemed to be torn from the bone. The boy sat, trancelike, holding it in place, his eyes fixed on his leg, and screamed with every breath.

It wasn't just the screaming itself that disturbed Maximus. Each scream contained a terrified howl for his mother. The boy must know that, if he didn't die first, he would soon be executed for rebellion; nailed to a wooden cross by his wrists and ankles. He would then spend his last few days in even more excruciating pain. The howl was driven by the youth's terror.

It had been about noon when two of Maximus' scouts

had spotted the four rebels resting beside a pool of water in the narrow desert wadi in which the stream that cut it flowed; the only water among miles of sand and rock. Eight of Maximus' more skilful soldiers had crept almost silently around the pool, between the valley wall and the reeds that grew at the water's edge. They had worked their way slowly upstream of the rebels to act as a cut-off group. The sheer rock walls of the valley would prevent any sideways escape away from the stream itself. It had taken those men nearly an hour to get into position, a piece of stealthy field craft that greatly impressed both Maximus and Cornelius Marcus Lucius, the other Roman-born officer with him. Once there was no escape either up or down the valley, a blast on a horn signalled the attack by the downstream assault group.

At the sudden sound the youngster had been on his feet and sprinting from the noise, only to be felled by the spear wielded by one of the cut-off group. At his screams and the appearance of the soldiers the three men had decided that resistance was pointless.

All four were dressed like every peasant Maximus saw in Judea, a one-piece linen undershirt that came down to their ankles and a mantle over the top. They all had head dresses, sensible for those living in the desert. The boy's clothes suggested a prosperous family while two others were obviously destitute. They smelled like they had been on the run for weeks and the dirt, wear and tears of their clothes told the same story. Those older two hadn't put up much of a fight. Maximus had seen birds offer more resistance to being caught for the pot and he judged that they lacked much knowledge of how to do so. They had surrendered their weapons, one a sword, the other a homemade spear. Now they sat doubtless numb with terror at their impending crucifixion too. At least they were silently numb though.

4

The leader of the band was different again. He was clearly a fighting man and his clothes were newer, though of humbler fabric than the boy's. He was evidently a more experienced desert dweller and had been armed with a stolen Roman sword and a concealed dagger. Maximus' troops also found a ready-made garrotte in a pouch on his belt. Despite the morale-sapping howls of the youth, which were slowly reducing his other companions to tears, his eyes were defiant and almost fanatical. Having drawn both his weapons at the horn blast he gave up as soon as the odds against them were obvious: no pointless sacrifice for him. He must know he is as good as dead too, thought Maximus, but clearly he will go to his cross resisting us.

Then one of the older men had called him "Barabbas". Maximus' troops had been patrolling the wilderness west of the Dead Sea for a week, part of operations mopping up remnants of the recent insurrection. Now they had captured a known zealot leader.

Maximus, forty and a father himself, looked at the wounded prisoner with both pity and weariness. The pity came from seeing yet another youngster, this one barely older than his own son, broken, facing death and crying for his mother. The weariness came from a week tramping through the Judean desert and cold nights trying to sleep on bare rock huddled in a blanket. He looked westwards at the April sun. Four hours to sunset he reckoned. He whistled across the pool. Lucius was talking to the decanus, Maximus' most senior non-commissioned officer, who had returned from leading a party to search further up the valley.

The men looked around at the whistle and Maximus made the infantry signals for 'Come to me' and at 'double marching'. They both hurried over in response.

'Centurion?' asked the decanus.

'I reckon we've got four hours 'til dusk, long enough to

5

get to the camp in the oasis at Ein Gedi tonight.' He jerked his thumb in the direction of the prisoners. 'The intelligence people there will want to meet Barabbas as soon as possible. That means a more comfortable night for us and proper food too.'

'Sounds good to me, Sir,' nodded the decanus, brightening at the thought. 'We're finished here.' He pointed towards a gap in the rocks through which water flowed towards them. 'We got less than a mile upstream. The spring that feeds this pool is barely three hundred yards away up there. Past that and there is sheer rock on three sides. The only big things upstream of here are lions.'

'Good,' Maximus turned to Lucius. 'Cornelius Marcus, would you take two sections ahead with Barabbas? Get to Ein Gedi as quickly as you can and tell them the rest of us are following with three more prisoners. Then could you make sure there's a good meal and a decent camp area waiting for us all when we get there?'

'Will do!' replied Lucius, also enthusiastic about a comfortable night.

'I'll assign you some men right away then, Sir,' the decanus said to Lucius, who nodded an acknowledgment.

Maximus then turned back to the decanus himself: 'I'll take the main body with the other prisoners now. You keep a section and sweep this place once more for anything else interesting. Then follow us down when you're done.'

'Yes, Centurion,' said the decanus. He turned away and started calling out commands. Around the valley soldiers began gathering equipment and falling into formation.

'A good day's work today, I think,' observed Maximus, grinning with satisfaction.

'I didn't know auxiliaries could work that well,' commented Lucius. A young officer of twenty, he was newly arrived from Rome on his first military posting. As a

Roman knight he had been hoping to find himself as a tribune in a legion but he lacked both a senatorial family background and experience in combat. Posted instead to an auxiliary unit in the guard of Pontius Pilate, the Prefect of Judea, he had barely concealed his disappointment to be working with auxiliaries, not proper legionaries.

'Well, they haven't quite the experience, or the professionalism, of Roman soldiers. But they do have local knowledge and enthusiasm; half of them were probably shepherds before they joined up.' Maximus chuckled and went on, 'They're used to creeping up on animals and they've probably all fought lions and wolves with their bare hands.' The two Romans laughed and, of course, Maximus' joviality contained much truth.

'What they lack in training they make up for in native wit and cunning, you mean?' Lucius asked. Maximus nodded.

'Something like that. Part of the Empire's success is that we use local talent.' Both were Roman citizens but Maximus, having risen through the ranks, thought that Lucius, like many young officers, tried to make up with ambition what he lacked in skill. The Centurion had always tried to make allowances for youngsters though: officers have to learn their trade somewhere and this was Lucius' first taste of life away from Rome. Maximus looked around at the soldiers, all suddenly energized at the thought of better food and sleep to come. 'Talent might not always be the right word though. Young ladies wouldn't encourage their fathers to bring too many of these men home to meet them, now would they?' They both laughed again.

'Right then, Cornelius,' he went on, 'You get away. Some creature comforts waiting when we get down to that oasis, please.' He looked again at the prisoners. The older three had noticed that something was happening, the boy was still screaming loudly. 'We'll need them if we've got to listen to that boy howling all the way back.'

CHAPTER 2

There were two great things about being Prefect of Judea, thought Pontius Pilate. He lay on a couch on a balcony facing the sea, savouring the fruity taste of some wine and picturing the Tuscan vineyards where the grapes had grown. He loved his face being caressed by the breeze off the sea and the warmth of the setting sun.

The first thing was this palace, a magnificent building by the last Judean king, Herod. For luxury and location it was the best in the land, with a relaxing view of the Mediterranean and the nearby harbour of Caesarea Maritima. The second was his accumulation of wealth, growing every day through various means: 'gifts' in return for favours, 'commissions' on trades, 'licence fees' for permission to operate different businesses and 'considerations' in return for 'patronage'. Maintaining law and order allowed everyone to flourish so, as the Roman Governor, he was entitled to a share of the proceeds from any venture that seemed likely to succeed. After all, if things went wrong, he was the one who would answer to the Emperor.

His mood suddenly darkened at the thought of the Emperor. His stomach clenched and his vision of Tuscan

9

vineyards was replaced by thoughts of his impending departure for Jerusalem to oversee the policing of the Passover festival. During the festival Jerusalem would be the most likely place for another insurrection to start. Top of his priorities were the number of violent contacts his troops had made recently with bands of Hebrew zealots which had amounted to a serious uprising. His own troops had contained the trouble but Passover was imminent. He knew there could be more. Being there meant he was close by in case of trouble but it was far from his favourite place to spend time.

Jerusalem was normally crowded and smelly, at least to a Roman nose. Every year Passover added about seventy thousand pilgrims, gripped by religious fervour, to the thirty thousand residents of Jerusalem. The recent uprisings had already increased the background political temperature and the risk of trouble. But the gods, it seemed, were keen to depress him even further. Just as his men had beaten one set of zealot troublemakers, his spies had reported that Jeshua the Nazarene, a dangerously popular and charismatic rabbi from Galilee, was expected to come to Jerusalem for the Passover festival.

It was normally politically useful to spend Passover there. Pilate would take Herod's palace in Jerusalem, just outside the Temple, party with the Romans and discreetly meet delegates from the Jewish council, the Sanhedrin. From his palace he could keep an eye on the celebrations, while trying to ignore the perpetual stench from the thousands of animals being slaughtered and burned in the Temple. If Jerusalem was already like a dry forest in a drought though, this Jeshua had the potential to light fires.

Pilate had about four thousand troops at his disposal and, an experienced soldier, he could take operational control if necessary. Though his officers were Romans, his soldiers were local auxiliaries and that was both a blessing and a curse. Simple hatred motivated them; so any lack as soldiers was regained by vindictiveness. Unfortunately though, the Hebrew fighters hated his troops equally ferociously, especially the Samaritans. Many had forgotten the cause of their centuries old religious dispute but hatred was still real and mutual. The bloodshed often had the vicious cruelty of civil warfare, magnifying the abuse and atrocity that accompanies any military occupation. A circle of increasing violence was always possible.

For now the troublemakers were scattered but he had been forced to consider asking Lucius Vitellus for reinforcements from his Roman Sixth Legion. Vitellus, Governor of Syria, was more senior and of higher social rank than Pilate and that would have made Pilate look incompetent. Apart from the humiliation of an ex-Praetorian officer like Pilate having to request help from the 'Ironclads', as the Sixth were known, it would have required Pilate to explain a failure to the Emperor Tiberius. A significant insurrection would, at best, extend his time here: 'the arsehole of the world' as one of his officers had called Judea, referring to the unpleasantly sulphurous gases given off by Asphaltites, the Dead Sea to the East.

He took another mouthful of wine, reflecting grimly how quickly the gods could arrange one's rise and fall. He had come to Judea several years earlier through the patronage of Lucius Aeilus Sejanus. Sejanus, though only an *eques* from the knightly class, like Pilate himself, was rapidly becoming Tiberius' enforcer and, in effect, his deputy. Sejanus had spotted Pilate, then a young officer serving (with some distinction, Pilate prided himself) in the German campaigns. Pilate had joined the elite Praetorian Guard, the Emperor's thousand-strong personal bodyguard just as Sejanus reorganised them into a unit criticised (and feared, the Praetorians were delighted to acknowledge) for fanatical loyalty to Tiberius.

Sejanus had arranged the Judea appointment. Pilate's star had been rising. He was newly married to Claudia Procula, a beautiful and highly intelligent daughter of the Proculis family, also knights of Rome. A successful governorship in a difficult province could lead to great things, Sejanus had assured him.

The storm that took Sejanus had come without warning. Had the downfall actually started a few years earlier when Sejanus had sought to marry above himself? The nobility had been appalled at an *eques* trying to marry the widow of Tiberius' son, Drusus. It was even whispered that Sejanus had actually arranged Drusus' poisoning. Perhaps Tiberius thought that Sejanus was overstepping the social mark: he had forbidden the match. It seemed another proof that Sejanus was glorying in sharing Tiberius' imperial status. Tiberius proved jealous.

Sejanus had shown stunned disbelief at the sudden arrival of a squad of Praetorians at his house with an accusation of treason. They killed Sejanus and his family moments later. The subsequent purge had killed many of his people too. News of Sejanus' disgrace had reached Judea quickly. A fellow ex-Praetorian and protégé of Sejanus had managed to leave on a long "research" trip to Syria and had later recounted this all to Pilate. They had sat on this very balcony, consoling themselves that being away from Rome they had escaped the storm, for now at least.

Pilate's job as Governor was, of course, exploiting Judea for the Emperor. It was a continual balancing act. Pilate extracted as much wealth as he could from the subject people. This lined Tiberius' treasuries and of course, Pilate's own pocket. The more Pilate could extract the better the Emperor would favour him and Judea had been relatively peaceful under his governorship so far. It was a success which should increase his chances of advancement under Tiberius's successor. Take too much wealth too fast, however and local leaders had less reason to prevent their lower orders from disrupting the smooth flow of commerce. Since his patron's death, Pilate worried less about fitting into a firmament of a new Emperor and more about preserving what he had. Even staying alive, perhaps.

CHAPTER 3

At a swish of silk he glanced over his shoulder as Claudia Procula, his wife, stepped onto the balcony. Pilate swung his feet onto the ground ready to stand but she sat on his lap first and kissed him on the mouth. She was warm to the touch and smelled of perfume. The silk of her dress caressed him and Pilate took time to enjoy the different sensations. She could tell he was troubled though and she frowned, then kissed him again with affection and gave him a slightly sarcastic grin.

'Is it that bad?'

'You know I hate Jerusalem at the best of times,' Pilate replied grumpily. 'I'm just coming to terms with a long journey to smell burned meat and sheep shit.'

'I know. But we'll be back here in a few weeks.'

'Yes, but this year Passover will be really stressful and we don't need any more trouble.'

'But you shouldn't need the Ironsides now, surely?' Claudia frowned a little. 'You've crucified dozens of the zealots in the last few weeks. We've got plenty of troops to keep on top of any left.'

'If only it were just the zealots. Just to make everything so much more unpredictable, your favourite holy man is coming to Jerusalem for Passover as well.'

'Who? Jeshua of Nazareth?' Claudia brightened up at the news.

'It's a distinct possibility, I'm told.' Pilate replied flatly. 'Why are you so excited? He's got all Galilee and Samaria talking about him. Actually, arguing about him is more accurate. Violence in Jerusalem when it's packed with pilgrims and the whole place could be in chaos. If Tiberius is still hunting for Sejanus' people, the last thing I need is a trip to explain to him why Judea is engulfed in civil war.'

'Jeshua isn't trying to start a civil war.' Claudia held out one hand to take a cup of wine from her slave and then waved her away with the other. The woman discreetly took up a position within hail in the room behind the balcony. 'He's strictly non-violent. That's what is so engaging about him, actually,' she said, sipping the wine. 'I've never heard him suggest breaking any law, let alone violent rebellion. If he was going to protest about anything, it'd be a silent protest.'

'Exactly!' said Pilate, 'they're the worst. Fighters are no trouble to us because we've got plenty of muscle. We can just kill anyone who draws a sword. The silent ones are the real troublemakers. I can't beat them with violence. Look what happened with those people when I showed off the standards we made to honour Tiberius.'

Claudia frowned at the memory. Newly into post some years earlier Pilate had placed some standards, honouring Tiberius Caesar, in the Antonia Fortress, next to the Temple in Jerusalem. They had contained symbols which the Hebrews had found idolatrous and highly offensive. A huge crowd had marched to Caesarea from Jerusalem and besieged Pilate's palace for days. Tired of deputations asking him for the standards' removal he finally decided to use force. The Hebrews were invited into the stadium in Caesarea which Pilate also filled with soldiers. Pilate heard their protest one more time, then, at a prearranged signal, his troops drew swords and advanced into the crowd. He gave the Hebrews a simple choice. Disperse peacefully or die there and then. After a shocked hesitation a leader of the protest had shouted that he preferred death and fell to the floor exposing his neck to the swordsmen next to him. The entire crowd copied him.

Pilate's troops would have liked nothing better than to kill dozens of people they hated anyway. Instead Pilate, fearing even more trouble from such an outcome, ordered the crowd's release. The humiliation was increased by having to publicly remove the standards as well. His stomach still churned with embarrassment whenever he remembered that day.

'You see?' Pilate taking her silence as accepting his point. 'Jeshua might revel in a confrontation with Rome that ends up killing him. What was his saying you told me about[1]? "Blessed are the meek"? That's because Jeshua knows that force is no use against the meek. Violence only works against scared and brutalised people with something to lose. He doesn't seem that scared. The meek wreak havoc against force. They just smile. To them, resorting to violence is just an admission of defeat.'

'I see what you mean.' Claudia sipped her wine in thought. 'But I still don't think Jeshua is out to cause trouble.'

'He doesn't need to be out to cause trouble,' replied Pilate. 'His whole view of life doesn't fit with the way this world works. Here's a for instance: turning the other cheek[2]? That's a calculated insult to the ruling class. You hit a slave who then "turns the other cheek" and he is telling you, to your face, that his authority to defy you is greater than your authority to beat him. That's how Jeshua sees it. If everyone started ignoring a master's right to… what was that other saying you told me about? "Lord it over others[3]"? Well, then the whole basis of punitive government would collapse. Jeshua doesn't live in the same world as us.'

'So it's not him causing trouble that worries you. It's other people fighting about what he says. Do you know he's coming?'

'No one is too sure but the High Priest seems worried. Why? Don't tell me you've got a soft spot for him.'

'Don't be silly!' Claudia laughed. 'But you know I find him interesting, perhaps because he does live in a different world. Quite a nice one too. He makes me think about life in a different way, that's all.'

'How nice to be free to think about different worlds. My worry is whether he's dangerous. What can I do if the worst I can threaten him with, in his eyes, is success?'

Pilate emptied his glass and signalled to a slave for more wine. Claudia looked at her husband and then brightened as an idea struck her.

'Are we going to stay with Nicodemus on the way to Jerusalem? Or are you hoping to do the entire trip in a day?'

'Sixty-odd miles in a day! Things aren't that bad. No. We will stay on Nicodemus' estate. Why?'

'Ask him for advice. He's friendly. He understands your problems as governor. But most importantly,' she smiled, relishing that she was going to impart something her husband clearly didn't know, 'he's a follower of Jeshua too. A discreet one given his position but if anyone can help you understand Jeshua, it will be him.'

CHAPTER 4

The Wadi Qelt, west of Jericho, Monday morning

'So who do *you* think I am, then,' asked Jeshua. 'John the Baptist back from the dead or the prophet Elijah out of the Scriptures perhaps?'

'Well, with all due respect, Rabbi, having only met you this morning I can't really say.' He'd built a successful fish-pickling business and Gad prided himself as a good salesman. His business supplied garum sauce to the Empire, as far as Rome itself. He had learned through experience that the best answer to any question was usually another question. 'Meeting you and your men in Jericho this morning was a great surprise. So how can anyone separate the real Jeshua of Nazareth from all the stories that quickly?'

'Good answer,' Jeshua smiled. 'And why does a Galilean like you travel to Jerusalem through Samaria? Especially with your wife.' Jeshua looked over his shoulder and nodded at Anna who was walking a few paces behind her husband. She looked down quickly to the ground in case her eyes caught Jeshua's and then glanced back up at Gad and smiled. 'Most Jews go along the coast to avoid the Samaritans, don't they?' finished Jeshua.

'I could ask you the same question about you coming

this way too, Rabbi,' Gad pointed out. 'The Wadi Qelt here is famously dangerous.' He glanced up at the sheer rock face towering above them on the right side of their path, itself barely wide enough for two men to walk side by side.

To their left was a steep river valley which ran through the barren hills of the Judean desert, already mostly dry with the days getting hotter as summer approached. With little water or vegetation this place had been called "the valley of the shadow of death" for centuries. On the other side of the valley was an aqueduct, built by the last king of Judea, Herod. It took water from the mountains down to Jericho on the flood plain of the Jordan River, already four hours walk behind them.

'We're going to meet my son Benjamin in Jerusalem for the Passover,' Gad went on. 'I have a friend in Jerusalem who acts as an export agent for me. We're all meeting at his home tomorrow. Benjamin went ahead with a shipment of garum a few days ago. He wanted to visit the Essenes at Qumran on the way. It's great meeting you by the way. He may be visiting them but we can now say we've travelled with the famous Jeshua of Galilee.' Gad smiled. 'He'll be so jealous when we tell him. We would have gone by the coast road but we left later than we had planned so we came this way too. I sometimes do, if I need to be fast. In troubled times like these there are usually merchants in Jericho and I always manage to find a few others wanting to band together.'

'We've been along here a few times and often with others,' agreed Jeshua. 'How's business?'

'The recent fighting has made life hard but in hard times you can usually work harder and make up some of the shortfall. And whatever else we think about the Romans they've given most people a taste for good garum. If I'd known Judea was still so violent though I would have told

Benjamin to go along the coast.

'If you make garum do you pickle the fish from the Lake of Galilee then?' asked Jeshua. 'You have probably done business with some of my people over the years.'

'I know at least two of the families of your men here,' Gad nodded. 'I was talking to them earlier as we left Jericho.' He paused wondering if he was about to be undiplomatic but, being a Galilean, he prided himself on straight talking. 'Their families aren't happy that they abandoned their businesses to follow you.'

'Oh I do understand that,' acknowledged Jeshua sadly. 'Some in my family feel the same about me. I'm the eldest son and everyone was shocked when I didn't take on my father's business when he died.'

'So are you going to lead Israel against the Romans then?' asked Gad. 'I've heard people say you are Elijah[4] and will bring fire down onto the heads of the Romans.'

'Just before he died my cousin, John, the Baptist, was in Herod Antipas' prison in Galilee. He sent some of his men asking similar questions. I sometimes wonder if John was hoping I'd overthrow that tyrant Herod and release him from prison. John wanted to know if I was the one Israel is waiting for too. Or should he tell his men to look for someone else[5].'

'Some say Herod might be God's anointed but others say that he's just a Roman puppet. Are you *messiah*?' asked Gad.

Jeshua looked at him for a couple of seconds before answering. Then he said: 'I told John's disciples to tell him that the blind saw again, the lame walked and the good news of God's kingdom is being shared with the poor.'

'Benjamin has a teacher among the Essenes. He told Benjamin that when *messiah* comes that is exactly what will happen.'

'So does that answer your question then?' asked Jeshua.

'It's the part with the poor that I think I struggle with,' admitted Gad.

'Oh? Why is that?'

'Didn't you once say that the rich would find it hard to get into the Kingdom?'

'I did. As a merchant familiar with loaded animals,' said Jeshua, 'you'll probably appreciate my image of the difficulty of a camel fitting through the eye of a needle[6]. I think it might prove a memorable phrase.'

'But aren't the rich blessed by God because they are worthy of the Kingdom? Isn't that why they're rich? If the rich aren't getting into the Kingdom what hope is there for the rest of us, especially the poor?'

'John the Baptist was my cousin, so he felt able to be more forthright with me than most. He was often worried that I was spending too much time with sinners. You are right that many respectable people see the sick and the destitute as cursed by God for their sins. Which is why I keep asking, for instance, how a girl whose husband has put her away is supposed to even eat, let alone have somewhere to live. All she has to sell is herself, so what chance has she got? Some people don't like answering that.'

'Putting women away without a proper divorce is always pretty despicable,' agreed Gad. 'Is that why you have women among your disciples?'

'Some people are often scandalised by the company I keep,' nodded Jeshua. 'We've a former tax collector and at least two zealots among my friends here, you know. Your brother Amos is out in front there with one of them, my friend Judah.' Jeshua pointed ahead to where, a few hundred yards along the path, two figures could be seen well ahead of the party. As scout, Judah's task was to spot an ambush, either of bandits or Roman soldiers, before the main group walked into it. 'Judah is still something of a zealot. He likes people to think his name 'Iscariot' comes from ancestors among the dagger-wielding *siccari*.'

Gad thought for a moment. 'I can see plenty of good people upset that sinners would be part of the Kingdom as well as themselves. What's the point of being good?'

'And like them many of my disciples feel that I should be making sinners suffer,' nodded Jeshua, 'especially the Romans and their collaborators in revenge for all our suffering. Judah is constantly upset when he thinks I spend too much time criticising the Pharisees, or the priests and scribes in the Temple. If you are in Jerusalem for Passover with us you will probably see Judah getting very angry with me.'

CHAPTER 5

Jerusalem, the Temple Mount, Monday evening

'You've noticed there are two types of lawyers, haven't you?' said Joseph tetchily, as he strode hurriedly through the gate on the west side of the Temple Mount and onto the bridge over the Tyropean Valley. 'Real courtroom advocates earn their fees speaking with precision,' continued the High Priest. 'Others clearly think their opinions command a premium for length.'

'I was wondering how much longer that Pharisee could go on,' agreed Jonathan, Captain of the Temple Guard, impressed that the High Priest could still deploy his icy wit. For over an hour they had both fought mounting frustration through a long and fruitless meeting in the Temple Court. An emergency meeting of Sanhedrin members, apparently to discuss a conjuring trick, simply showed panic.

Joseph Caiaphas and his father-in-law, Annas, son of Seth, were already planning how to deal with Jeshua. Annas and his family were among the Sadducee aristocrats who were wealthy enough to maintain themselves as High Priests of the Temple in Jerusalem. In fact Annas had been Joseph's predecessor, replaced years earlier on the instructions of Pilate's predecessor, Valerius Gratus, now retired in Rome. Their experience of the intrigues of power and politics equipped them to deal with minor difficulties, such as troublesome prophets, and without too much public fuss.

'Fortunately priestly training includes maintaining gravitas in the face of idiocy. Along with a believable smile.' Joseph glanced at his subordinate and raised his eyebrows knowingly. Accompanied by guards and torchbearers the longest-serving High Priest in recent years was now late for dinner. They strode quickly along the road that connected the Temple Mount with the wealthy quarters of Jerusalem where the High Priest's house was situated.

'It's probably easy enough to arrange tricks in which apparently dead bodies come back to life,' Joseph observed as they marched, 'but three weeks before Passover, I can't think of a less welcome arrival in Jerusalem than Jeshua the Galilean troublemaker. He must know how awkward he makes things.'

'The four days between Lazarus' death and Jeshua raising him from his tomb[7] was a nice touch,' Jonathan commented. 'It makes it much harder to explain as a conjuring trick. Perhaps sorcery is a more likely explanation?'

'Whether sorcery is more likely or not is hardly the issue,' Joseph explained. 'Everyone knows the dead do not rise again, so word of Jeshua's latest wonder will be round the city by now and round the whole country by tomorrow night. That's the issue! Why couldn't he have stayed up north in Galilee?'

'There have been rumours for weeks that Jeshua was coming back to Jerusalem,' said Jonathan. 'That was always going to be like a fox arriving in a hen house.'

'That's an understatement!' Joseph harrumphed, 'Jerusalem is filling with Passover pilgrims and becoming increasingly combustible. Half the mob thinks Jeshua is the prophet Elijah himself, straight back out of the Scriptures!'

'I gather the Tetrarch of Galilee thinks Jeshua might be John the Baptist,' Jonathan said almost as an aside, 'back from the dead too.' There was an unmistakeable grin in his voice.

'Good!' said Joseph venomously. 'Then Herod Antipas will be preoccupied with worrying whether Jeshua is coming to get him. Hopefully he'll hide in his palace during Passover. Not having to dine with the murderous little despot would be a blessing.' Joseph shuddered at the memory of John's recent beheading by Antipas at a particularly debauched party.

'Do you think there is a danger that the people might see Jeshua as another Maccabee in the making?' asked Jonathan.

Joseph sniffed dismissively but then considered the idea for a moment. 'Well, when the Maccabees overthrew Antiochus Epiphanes and the Syrians, they cleaned the corrupt from the Temple organisation and set up a Hebrew state too. Some seem to be hoping Jeshua will do the same.'

'But if they think he's *messiah*, could he threaten us as well?'

'Jeshua? The anointed one?' Joseph snorted with ridicule. 'Why would it please the Lord, the God of Abraham, to choose a jobbing builder? Especially one from Galilee?'

'Many of the prophets were humble men,' pointed out Jonathan.

'Prophets, yes. Occasionally,' Joseph paused. Then he went on: 'I could accept Jeshua might be a prophet, even with his lifestyle.'

'I've often wondered how such a disagreeable individual can criticise us, or the Pharisees,' agreed Jonathan 'He's upset our friend back there in court, for sure.'

'He'll upset many more if he causes any trouble,' Joseph

replied 'especially if he upsets the Romans,' he added emphatically. 'That old joke "Has anything good ever come from Nazareth[8]?" could suddenly acquire a very sombre slant. The Romans are still chasing the last bunch of zealots who attacked them. He must have noticed the bodies of the rebels they've crucified rotting along the roadsides from here to Samaria?'

Over his years in power Joseph had watched several *'messiahs'* lead bands of misguided and desperate fools against the military might of Rome. Jeshua seemed an unusually clever, articulate and subversive teacher though. He might well be a credible figurehead. His dangerous ability to construct spectacular "signs and wonders" was also disturbing. Only that evening he had arrived in a nearby village, without any warning, and supposedly raised a man called Lazarus, who had died a few days earlier, from his tomb. This was only the latest and there were other legends too.

'You know, between you and me,' Joseph said quietly to Jonathan, 'I wonder occasionally what I should do if *messiah* does arrive while I'm High Priest.'

'You don't really think Jeshua could be *messiah* after all, do you?' asked Jonathan in a surprised tone.

'Keep your voice down,' Joseph glanced around at the torchbearers who seemed to have heard nothing. 'Of course I don't.'

'But have you actually considered it?' asked Jonathan.

'It was the reports about what the people were *saying* about Jeshua that posed me the question,' replied Joseph. 'You know that story about the Persian *magi* coming to visit him when he was born[9], for instance?'

'The astrologers? Yes, I've heard the story?'

'Astrologers, among other things,' nodded Joseph. 'There's a story that his birth coincided with a conjunction of stars and planets, in Aries, heralding an unusually important royal event. Aries being Judea's controlling house, thirty-odd years ago stars rising like that brought them to Judea to find the new king.'

'But we wouldn't get involved with astrology, would we?' asked Jonathan.

'Of course not but as one of my scribes pointed out,' Joseph explained, 'if it is true, then Beelzebub's arts might dance to the Lord Almighty's tunes after all. You weren't born at the time but Antipas' father, King Herod, slaughtered hundreds of baby boys in Judea to eliminate the supposed usurper[10]. Murderousness is obviously inherited.'

'But Jeshua's lifestyle as a holy man seems anything but holy.'

'Hence my questions rather than any answers,' agreed Joseph. 'We will just have to trust that when it pleases the Lord to send his anointed, he will make it blindingly obvious.' They had reached the Palace, built by King Herod, which Pontius Pilate occupied when he came to Jerusalem. 'I trust the Prefect has yet to arrive?'

'He's still in Caesarea Maritima but due any day,' replied Jonathan.

'Good,' Joseph glanced up at the battlements above them. 'One thing worse than a spoiled dinner would be giving Pilate the satisfaction of seeing me hurrying anywhere.'

CHAPTER 6

Jerusalem, the High Priest's house, Monday evening

Joseph's slaves opened the torch-lit doors of his residence as his party approached. Once inside they helped him remove the cloak that covered his robes. He nodded an acknowledgment to the news that Annas had already arrived from the meeting and was accompanied by another guest as expected. Dinner was ready whenever he wished.

In his changing room his valet helped him wash, then dress him in fresh robes ready for the meal. Having checked himself in a mirror, he strode through the house to an antechamber on the upper floor beyond which lay a small dining room. Jonathan turned from a tapestry that he had been admiring; Annas rose from the couch on which he had been reclining while talking to another younger man. Annas embraced Joseph, kissing him on both cheeks.

'That meeting was something of a bore,' said Annas sonorously. 'That rabbi makes the Pharisees rather nervous.' Then he added a note of humorous irony: 'You did sound so very sincere in taking their concerns so very seriously. Anyway, let me introduce Eleazar, son of Daniel, the lawyer I think will be able to help us.' The younger man had also risen when Joseph entered the room and now stepped forward.

'Ah, yes. Eleazar! My father-in-law speaks very highly of your professional skills and I hear your fame as an advocate is growing rapidly. You are in the Sanhedrin quite often, I think?' The scent of money about Eleazar reminded Joseph how rarely the words "poor" and "lawyer" went together. Joseph noted his hair and beard were cut and trimmed into a modest style and his mantle was unadorned but beautifully cut of fine cloth.

'Its very kind of you to say so, Sir,' smiled Eleazar modestly. 'I do seem to be establishing a good practice as a criminal lawyer.'

'Some might wonder if there is any other kind of lawyer,' quipped Joseph. There was laughter for a few moments and Eleazar smiled.

'I seem to be able to help the victims of potential injustices,' he said in dignified tones, 'although sadly at the moment the Romans are creating injustice rather faster than we can deal with it. I see you in the Sanhedrin all the time but I'm honoured that you recognised me.'

'We met at the Tetrarch's palace recently too,' said Joseph, 'but I think the least said of *that* dinner the better.'

'Indeed so,' nodded Eleazar with a suitable look of distaste. 'A shocking climax to what was otherwise quite an occasion.'

Annas and Jonathan already knew Eleazar quite well and so there was more small talk about friends, family and assorted business contacts as drinks were offered. Eleazar, Joseph noted, hung on the words of those talking, asking questions that indicated he had actually understood what they had said. Charming, modest and set for great things, he was an ideal choice for any Hebrew girl, Joseph decided. He mused that he would be happy for Eleazar to meet his own daughters and suspected his daughters would also be delighted to meet him.

Joseph's steward quietly indicated to his master that dinner was served.

'I know we've been rather dismissive of the Pharisees who called that Sanhedrin meeting in such haste this evening but, let us be frank,' said Joseph as he showed his guests through a pair of double doors into the adjoining dining room, 'Jeshua can cause the Temple as much trouble as he can cause the Pharisees. Any serious insurrection threatens us all. The Romans might close the Temple if they thought we instigated any violence. Can you imagine being forced into worshipping Caesar as Lord? That's what the Romans require from the most of the Empire's subjects, you know,' he pointed out in an ominous tone.

Joseph indicated the separate couches that encircled a long, low table. Each man stood as Joseph gave thanks to God for the food and then they sat down.

'I'm starving!' he said as he signalled to the steward who in turn summoned two more slaves with platters of food, which they placed on the table. Two others served each man with wine and water. When they had finished Joseph indicated to the steward that they were to be left alone. The steward ushered his subordinates out and followed them, closing the doors behind him. Then the four men started to take food onto their own dishes.

'Jeshua is not good news for any of us,' Joseph continued. 'While he's just a rabbi in the north, or even in the deserts by the Dead Sea, he's really no more of a problem than the Essenes are in Qumran. But if he preaches subversion in the Temple Courts at the Passover? Much more serious!' He swept his hands over the meal before them. 'I hope the food is still fresh.'

'I'm sure your chef will have coped with the delay.' Annas assured him, his mouth already full of some fish. 'I've always envied you him.'

The men ate, almost in silence, for a few minutes. Then Joseph tossed a chicken bone onto a plate and said: 'As I mentioned to the meeting, if necessary, it is better that one man dies than the nation is destroyed,' his voice coughed slightly before he continued, 'but do we actually want him dead?'

'It is a bit extreme,' nodded Annas, frowning. 'Can't we just lock him up over Passover? Even pay him to stay in the desert? After all, if we killed every Hebrew with radical ideas there wouldn't be many of us left. In a sense we *habiru* have been everybody's misfits since the dawn of time.'

'He will have lots of support in Jerusalem come the Passover,' observed Jonathan. 'My agents report he's got plenty of followers here, including some very powerful people. He is popular with the mob too. There would be trouble unless we could charge him with something convincing.'

'Jeshua staying in the desert would be fine,' said Joseph, nodding his acknowledgement of Annas' point. 'People sitting in the desert muttering about purity are just that: in the desert. The Temple is where the Hebrew people worship the Lord. If some philosophers and zealots feel better moaning in the wilderness then we are spared having to listen to them here.'

'The Baptist stayed in the desert,' smiled Jonathan, 'and caused himself rather a lot of trouble.'

'True,' chuckled Joseph. 'But what trouble did he cause us? He told lots of people they should repent of their sins and live better lives before God. That's fine by me.' Joseph reached out and took a bunch of grapes.

'The fool probably didn't bargain on losing his head,' laughed Annas.

Joseph chewed and swallowed his grapes. 'But not because he told the people to live godly lives. Insulting the

Tetrarch, or his women, is never a good move.' The men laughed at their memory of Herod Antipas' discomfort. 'It was getting tangled in the Tetrarch's vanity that killed him.'

'So if Jeshua stays in the desert he would have your blessing, then?' asked Eleazar.

'So long as he sticks to telling people to do Torah better,' replied the High Priest. 'I am not even that worried if he casts the odd aspersion on the Temple, so long as he doesn't actually come and cast any here.'

'So his teaching isn't really subversive in your eyes?'

'Telling people to do Torah better? No. Suggesting we should be truer in our worship in the Temple? Of course not, But that's not his real message.' Joseph mood darkened. 'He's much more subtle than that. If he comes to Jerusalem conjuring up signs,' he tapped a finger on the table for emphasis, 'which everyone takes as a claim to be *messiah* then he's dangerous, especially if he turns up at Passover.' He looked at the others to emphasise his point before he went on.

'"Let those who have ears hear[11]", he says,' Joseph waved a hand for emphasis. 'Well I can hear what he's saying. His stories tell us with ears to hear that he thinks he is the anointed fulfilling Scripture.'

'He wouldn't be the first though,' pointed out Eleazar quietly. 'Unless he really is the *messiah*, his time will pass. Just like the rest, no one will ever hear of him again. Why not just let nature take its course?'

Joseph drew a deep breath as he thought about his answer and glanced at Annas. Eleazar had yet to fully understand the problem. 'Jeshua threatens us in a number of ways. He could disrupt the flow of sacrifices at a peak time. He could also create a major breakdown of public order. That in turn might provoke the Romans to take violent action, which could lead to bloodshed. Even worse, if the Romans considered such discontent seditious, they might use it as a precedent to curtail our freedom to worship in the Temple. The real horror of course, would be Jeshua and the zealots attacking the Romans. That would unleash incalculable consequences.'

'Is it his coming to Jerusalem at Passover that makes it so difficult?' Eleazar asked.

'The city is filled with pilgrims,' nodded Joseph. 'For many this will be their only visit to Jerusalem for a major festival. If they lose confidence in us and decide to follow Jeshua, the zealots, or both, the consequences are unpredictable. The more so now given the recent uprising.'

Annas nodded and waved a piece of bread in Eleazar's direction. 'Look at who he travels with, Eleazar,' said Annas with his mouth still full. He chewed and swallowed the mouthful, then continued: 'Fishermen, tax collectors, sick people. He's even got Samaritans with him; that's almost dabbling with foreign faiths! The Lord only knows how many lepers and whores are with him now. I bet he's all but married to that crazy woman who had demons. In fact it's a disgrace that he's not properly married at his age.' He paused then went on; 'Imagine what they're doing on the cold nights by the campfire.'

'I think he is trying to create a different Israel from ours,' said Jonathan, 'and he'll fill it with all the wrong sort of people.'

'Exactly,' agreed Joseph, nodding vigorously at Jonathan, then looking back to Eleazar. 'Take those supposed healings as an example: He doesn't just heal people, he says he forgives them. That's blasphemy! Only the Lord Almighty can forgive.' Joseph tore up some bread with evident irritation and wiped some sauce from his plate.

Jonathan reinforced the High Priest's point: 'They wouldn't be sick or disabled if they weren't sinners, would they? By claiming authority to forgive he's effectively proclaiming a new Exodus story. A new "People of God". In his Exodus story he seems to be both the Land of Israel and the Temple himself. That's what all his "Kingdom of God" business is about. We are effectively exiles in our own land and he's claiming to be the end of exile.'

'I can see why the Pharisees are so scandalised then,' commented Eleazar. 'Once when he was here before I remember the Pharisees investigating a blind man who claimed Jeshua had mixed up some mud and put it on his eyes to cure his blindness. And on the Sabbath too[12]. Needless to say that prompted some comment. They couldn't believe that a man from God would do such a thing on the Sabbath. Some thought that that made Jeshua a sinner as well.'

'I remember that,' said Jonathan. 'Wasn't the man lying? I thought he hadn't been blind in the first place?'

'That was why the enquiry summoned his parents. They confirmed that he had been blind from birth but they refused to say how their son could see now. Of course, that might have been to do with the fact that anyone saying Jeshua was anointed would be expelled from the synagogue. They told us to ask their son. He wouldn't be drawn on whether Jeshua was a sinner and just said "I was blind but now I can see."'

'So what happened?' asked Annas.

'He refused to change his story and the Pharisees said he was Jeshua's disciple. Then he got pretty rude actually. The Pharisees pointed out that they didn't know where Jeshua came from. He said that if Jeshua wasn't from God he could have done nothing.'

'I doubt that when down well with the Pharisees,' laughed Jonathan.

'It didn't,' agreed Eleazar. 'They said he'd been born in

sin and how dare he think of teaching them anything. Then they threw him out of the synagogue. They still can't see how someone claiming to be from God can ignore the Sabbath law like that. The man was obviously a sinner since he's been blind from birth.' He paused for a moment. 'Obviously the most important thing now is to safeguard the Hebrew people. Could you prosecute Jeshua for blasphemy? Or even deception? Unless he is *messiah* he's deceiving the people.'

'Trouble is, the claim to be *messiah* is the dangerous part,' said Annas quietly, 'because the end of exile is what our people are crying out for. You said it earlier, injustice is everywhere. Plenty already think he is *messiah*. Execute him and many will say we're murdering God's anointed and extending our exile. Doing so in Jerusalem at Passover could inflame the mob. Then we've the same problem with the Romans.'

'But if the Romans thought he was undermining *their* rule,' Joseph smiled grimly, 'wouldn't they execute him?' The others thought quietly for a moment.

'Well, he does talk about building a new kingdom,' Annas observed.

'If we demonstrate to the Romans that he is a zealot challenging the Emperor,' asked Jonathan. 'and our people realise he's misleading the nation with trickery or sorcery, like today, will they accept his execution?'

'I think so,' replied Joseph.

'I think you're onto something,' said Annas, he stroked his beard for a moment then continued: 'But Joseph, Passover gives you enough worries. Leave dealing with Jeshua to us. I'm sure we can find some people to testify to him working to create this new kingdom of his.'

'Thank you,' said Joseph. 'Jonathan, do we know where he is now?'

'Yes,' replied Jonathan. 'He's in Bethanya tonight. I can get men there to arrest him at first light if you want. Otherwise he'd probably escape in the dark.'

Arresting Jeshua near Jerusalem risked unrest given the excitement over Lazarus, thought Joseph. On the other hand, getting Jeshua safely out of circulation before Jerusalem filled with excitable pilgrims, and nervous soldiers, had much to commend it. In any case, he already had plenty to worry about in the Temple at Passover without Jeshua lighting political tinder as well.

'Jonathan, what about the Romans?' asked Annas. 'They might wonder why a large party of our guards are suddenly leaving Jerusalem in the dark.'

'Don't worry. I can make sure their sentries don't take alarm. I'm meeting the Roman garrison command group tomorrow morning. I'll say it was an exercise to confirm that we can respond to trouble quickly.'

Joseph thought for a few moments, then he made up his mind. 'If we can, let's arrest him now.'

CHAPTER 7

Jerusalem, the Temple Mount, Tuesday noon

The sun was nearly at its midday zenith when Jonathan, this time with one of his officers, crossed the bridge across the Tyropean Valley and onto the Temple Mount deep in conversation. They parted company in the Court of the Gentiles. The officer, who had led the operation to Bethanya the night before, went to his quarters while Jonathan walked on, deep in thought, through the colonnades under the buildings that housed the offices of the High Priest.

The party that had gone to Bethanya had returned empty-handed. Its leader had met Jonathan to brief him as he left the Antonia Fortress after his meeting with the Romans. Joseph would not have been overly perturbed by the news that Jeshua had not been there to be arrested. Joseph though was focused on the religious formalities of the Passover. Jonathan was now working on the Jeshua problem with Annas. As he entered the offices Jonathan decided his anxiety was because he didn't really know Annas, nor could he guess at his reaction.

Jonathan now slightly regretted not going himself, even though he had entrusted the mission to a competent officer, by popular agreement the best of his immediate subordinates. The party had been large enough to overcome any realistic levels of opposition but there had actually been no trouble because there had been neither Jeshua nor many obvious supporters in Bethanya. Jonathan had been at the final briefing before dawn when the Temple guards had set out from Jerusalem. The plan to encircle Bethanya had been a good one. No civilian had entered or left the village through the cordon. The village had been searched thoroughly and the locals interviewed. Some, including a couple of Galileans, were still being interrogated about Jeshua's whereabouts. Jonathan's own presence would not have affected the outcome. Though a model operation, the mission had failed to arrest Jeshua simply because the rabbi had not been there.

He was not entirely certain that Jeshua had even stayed in Bethanya the night before, though the villagers were suspiciously contradictory. Some claimed never to have seen him in their lives and didn't know who the soldiers were talking about. Some had assured the troops that Jeshua had left after the incident at Lazarus' tomb the evening before, others that he had left before dawn. Some claimed the celebrations for Lazarus' return to life had clouded their memories. The mission leader's assessment was that Jeshua had left with a group of his closest supporters during the night and had headed into the desert, probably back towards Jericho.

Jonathan's officer had sent a scouting party to Jericho through the Wadi Qelt but they would be hours behind Jeshua and he didn't think there was much chance they would find him. Another party was heading to Qumran, in case Jeshua intended to lie low with the Essenes. Jonathan thought it was worth a try but he knew Jeshua didn't really get on with the Essenes. Even without the connivance of the locals there were plenty of hiding places in the wilderness anyway. Nothing was Jonathan's fault, but the easiest question from a superior looking to blame a subordinate was to ask about his location during the mission in question.

Instead he had attended a rather tricky meeting with the Roman commanders in the Antonia Fortress. Its stated aim was to review the security arrangements in Jerusalem for the forthcoming Passover festival but dominating the discussion was the impending arrival of Pontius Pilate in a few days time. The Romans were curious about the party of Temple guards that had hurriedly left Jerusalem before dawn to carry out a "cordon and search" of Bethanya. They were also annoyed that they had known nothing about it. Most suspicious was Pilate's Chief of Staff, who had arrived overnight from Caesarea Maritima. Jonathan had assured him it had simply been a precautionary exercise to confirm that the Temple Guards could arrest troublemakers without inflaming the situation, should the need arise, during the festival.

Jonathan wasn't certain that the Roman had bought the cover story. Wasn't it normal to inform the garrison of any paramilitary operations in advance and in good time? Hadn't Jonathan thought through the potential consequences of Roman troops mistaking a legitimate Temple operation for a zealot attack, particularly given the security situation following the recent uprising? If it had just been an exercise, Pilate's Chief of Staff had asked him pointedly, why the prisoners? Jonathan had known he was on shaky ground but had smiled calmly in reply. He was informing them now because the exercise had been to test out the rapid response. Notifying the Romans might have warned his own men of the exercise.

If a troublemaker comes to light we will have to move that fast to catch him, Jonathan had bluffed. Warning in advance might not always be possible, so it had been important to practice doing things in a way which the Romans would have seen as legitimate. The Romans guards had reported it correctly, hadn't they? We shouldn't need to repeat it, he reminded the Roman commanders. It had confirmed that such an operation could be launched, without deadly mistakes, in the dark.

The frown on Centurion Maximus' face and the undisguised hostility from Pilate's deputy suggested that they were still unhappy but there was the imminent arrival of the Prefect to attend to and, to Jonathan's relief, the meeting had moved on.

Jonathan was shown into a small anteroom in the High Priest's suite of offices. A slave brought in a platter with a jug of pomegranate juice and two cups, leaving them on a table against a wall. He bowed to Jonathan and left the room, closing the doors behind him. Jonathan poured himself a cup of juice and sipped it quietly. Seconds later the doors swung open and in swept Annas.

'Morning, Jonathan,' he announced briskly and brightly. 'Excellent dinner last night, don't you think, despite the delay. My son-in-law speaks very highly of your team but I gather the hunters missed their prey this morning.'

'I'm afraid so,' replied Jonathan, 'By the time we got there Jeshua had already left.'

'I don't think he will have gone to Qumran,' said Annas. 'Don't you think he's more likely to have gone back east of the Jordan?'

Jonathan wondered who might have already briefed Annas. 'I agree that Jeshua will either head east over the Jordan River, or north back to Galilee. Which one depends on his intentions. If he wants to be here for the Passover festival, though, he'll probably hide nearby. Hence the party heading to Qumran. My officer felt it was the most likely of the obvious alternatives and he had the manpower with him. We might be lucky. On the other hand Jeshua may decide there is now too much danger here and be heading home to Galilee. He's obviously a shrewd man.'

Annas looked out of the window at the crowds that were milling around in the courtyard below. He stroked his beard thoughtfully and then turned back to Jonathan.

'He has more options than we have resources at the moment, doesn't he?'

'I'm afraid so, Sir,' replied Jonathan. 'The High Priest is right that Jeshua is no threat if he's in the desert.' Jonathan smiled adding: 'and that would include a social desert like Galilee.' They both laughed. The bumbling Galileans were the subjects of many Judean jokes.

'The trouble will be if he returns to Jerusalem,' Jonathan continued. 'I'm sending some agents out to try to see if we can pick up news of his whereabouts. He draws huge crowds, so he shouldn't be too hard to hear about. Do we still want to arrest him if he's a long way away?'

'If he's at a safe distance we'll leave him for now. We can't scatter men all over the country and properly police the Temple at Passover as well. Tell them to keep him in sight. Then we'll discuss it once the festival is over.'

'Very good, Sir,' said Jonathan. 'I am also putting a patrol on the roads into Jerusalem to try to pick him up if he returns here in the next few days.'

'Good idea,' Annas smiled at Jonathan. 'Don't forget discretion is needed too. How did the Romans take the news of our exercise?'

'I was reprimanded for not telling them in advance,' replied Jonathan, smiling again. 'The usual stuff about wanting to avoid people getting hurt if things get dramatic by mistake. Pilate's Chief of Staff had arrived last night and fussed about loads of minor detail. He's either new in the job or was just in a really bad mood.'

'Good! Did they seem worried about Jeshua?' asked Annas.

'No. They didn't mention him and I wasn't going to raise the subject.'

'Let's try to keep it that way. You've a contact in the garrison, haven't you?'

'Yes, I am on quite good terms with one of their centurions. If Jeshua becomes a concern for them, I'll hear about it through him.'

'Excellent! Well it's good that we've scared him off. Hopefully he will go back to Galilee. If he returns, try to take him before he gets into the city.' Then Annas thought for a few seconds. 'He pulls off a huge conjuring trick and then vanishes, so he clearly has influential friends here. Try and find someone close to him who will work with us if he does come back.'

CHAPTER 8

Jerusalem, the Antonia Fortress, Tuesday early afternoon

Maximus placed his sword, in its scabbard, and his helmet, with its distinctive side-to-side centurion's plume, on the table just inside the door of his office in the Antonia Fortress. In his past in the legions he had served in Germany and there had been days in the northern winters when he would have given anything to be warm. In the mid-day heat of Jerusalem he often struggled to remember how cold could be anything but a pleasure. Even in April, at noon it had been a hot walk back to the Antonia Fortress after checking preparations for Pilate's arrival at the Herodian Palace. His slave helped him out of his breastplate then Maximus peeled off his sweaty undershirt and dried himself before tossing the shirt and the towel back at the slave. He accepted a dry shirt in return and a cup full of mixed fruit juice and water. He gulped it down, the slave refilled the cup and, after a small bow, left the room as Maximus sat down at his desk and glanced at the work which awaited him.

Lucius poked his head round the door and waved a scroll: 'Intelligence summaries for the days we've been away.' Then he came to his real point of interest: 'That was an interesting meeting wasn't it?'

Maximus smiled grimly as he looked up and waved to the young man to enter.

He knew Lucius slightly resented this posting in Judea, a country with little social grace. Lucius eventually wanted a command in the elite Praetorian Guard in Rome but Maximus refrained from comment when Lucius mentioned it. Nothing wrong with ambition, Maximus thought, but to be an officer in the Praetorians you had to be excellent at your job and politically astute too.

Maximus had once met the infamous and ruthlessly-focused Sejanus, lately the Praetorian Prefect. You'd be hard pressed to pack all Sejanus' victims into one graveyard, Maximus had quietly pointed out to Lucius. With Tiberius old and less than healthy, the mighty were already jockeying for positions when he died. Rome could be a dangerous place: even Sejanus had pushed his own political ambitions too far.

'Pilate's Chief of Staff wasn't very happy with Temple police launching night-time raids without telling us, was he?' said Lucius and added, with a faint trace of annoyance: 'Jonathan embarrassed the garrison which means the Prefect's eyes will be on us too I suppose.'

'We certainly don't need people thinking that we aren't in control of the city,' nodded Maximus.

'You understand the Hebrews, don't you? What was Jonathan up to?'

'You mean launching the raid in the first place,' replied Maximus, 'or giving us a load of horse-shit about why?'

'Both, I suppose.'

Maximus abandoned any immediate idea of work and thought for a few moments. 'Jonathan's pretty straight. I can't see him trying to fool us unless he thinks he's got good reason. Maybe it really was an exercise to test his troops' readiness. But then, he wouldn't normally just forget to tell us.'

'So what might appear a good reason to him then?'

'Nothing I can immediately think of,' replied Maximus shaking his head. Then he pointed at the scroll in Lucius' hand. 'What happened in our absence, then?'

'Not much,' replied Lucius who had read the reports already. 'Another patrol also had a contact with a band of zealots. They're pursuing them into the desert to the East. With luck they'll track them to a base camp. The most unusual thing was a magician playing a trick with a dead body out at Bethanya. Apparently he made the chap who'd died come back to life. Some of the religious people got agitated and the Sanhedrin members sat late. Nothing of any military significance though.'

'In Bethanya?' Maximus raised his eyebrows. 'That was where Jonathan's raid went. Here's a long odds bet for you, Jeshua of Nazareth was involved, wasn't he?'

CHAPTER 9

Lucius undid the scroll and scanned the reports quickly. Then he exclaimed: 'You're right, the conjuror was from Nazareth and was called Jeshua.' Lucius looked at Maximus enquiringly. 'How did you know?'

'You've heard of John the Baptist?'

'A zealot, wasn't he? Didn't Herod Antipas kill him for upsetting one of his mistresses?'

Maximus winced slightly at Lucius' lack of discretion. 'I wouldn't suggest you put it quite like that, given Antipas is Tetrarch of Galilee and our proxy there. No, the Baptist wasn't a zealot but Jeshua is like him. Based in Capernaum. Orator, storyteller, draws huge crowds. He stays mainly up in the north. People say he does healings. Brought a Pharisee's girl back to life once, they say. In fact one of our centurions in Capernaum[13] claimed Jeshua brought one of his slaves back to life. Hence my guess that it was Jeshua.'

'From up north? So Jeshua's a Galilean too?' asked Lucius

'He is from Galilee but they say he's a Judean,' Maximus continued. 'He's still got relatives in Bethlehem but, among the stories is that his parents weren't married when he was born. Perhaps his family aren't too keen on the association, I don't know, but maybe that's why he stays with people in Bethanya when he's here. He's got quite powerful friends here too, some in the Sanhedrin. He's only a builder but he's always attracted interest from the high and mighty.'

'Really? Why?'

'For a start when he was born there was a very rare conjunction of stars, significant enough to get some leading scholars trekking all the way from the Euphrates to find a new King. King Herod of Judea, the present Tetrarch of Galilee's father, had hundreds of little boys killed trying to do away with him. You could say Jeshua's been upsetting the powers-that-be since birth.'

'A healer is a useful chap to have about, especially if he can bring you back to life if he gets to you too late.' Lucius laughed and Maximus smiled too.

'The Jews are waiting for an anoninted one. A new king, if you like. One who will revive Israel and purify the land by ejecting us unclean gentiles from west of the Jordan River. They believe this land is theirs by divine gift.

'I've noticed they're insufferably superior,' nodded Lucius.

'Exactly,' went on Maximus. 'Well, many see illness as God's curse for a bad life. So when Jeshua cures some pretty disreputable people, including pagan soldiers, that undermines some of the worthies' self-righteousness. The ancient Hebrew prophets actually say God's anointed one will free the world from the curse of death and rule a new age of peace. But some rich folks don't like the thought that their God might include poor folks.'

'Does Jeshua think he's this anointed one?' Lucius thought for a moment: 'You know, the poet Virgil was lyrical about a new golden age too, wasn't he? How does the poem go: "the goats will come home with milk-filled udders…serpents will perish and poison will be no more"? Or something like that. I'm not that good at poetry.'

Mainly self-taught, Maximus took great pride in being

47

literate and was quite impressed. Perhaps Cornelius Lucius had a more civilised side to go with his youthful arrogance.

'Well then, here's something else that might interest you, Cornelius,' said Maximus. 'There is a legend about Jeshua: his mother was visited by the gods. God, actually; the Jews only believe in one. She became miraculously pregnant with Jeshua[14].'

'I bet that went down well with her family!' snorted Lucius. 'Imagine how her father reacted when he found out. Don't they kill girls here who get pregnant out of marriage?'

'It's been known,' nodded Maximus. 'Apparently her betrothed married her anyway. Lucky for her. Have you ever read the Hebrew writer Isaiah? It's in Greek now, as well as Hebrew.'

'Can't say I have,' said Lucius shaking his head.

'Well he talks about *messiah* too, that's the Hebrew for anointed.' Maximus frowned as he tried to remember a verse or two. '"The people that walked in darkness have seen a great light. To us a son is born, a child is given and the government will be upon his shoulders. He will be the Mighty God, the Everlasting Father and the Prince of Peace[15]."'

'Is that a quote?'

'More or less. It's the gist of it. I've got the scroll somewhere, if you want. You read Greek?'

'Yes, of course, but that's alright. I get the picture. Wasn't Virgil also writing about Augustus Caesar though? I thought it was just figurative? Is this Isaiah saying this anointed one is the same as the Emperor? If the Jews are planning a challenge to our Empire shouldn't we have words with this Isaiah?'

'Oh, Isaiah lived centuries ago,' said Maximus disarmingly. 'Now the Jews are expecting a man who will re-establish their nation. I have heard people wonder if the

48

legend of Jeshua's miraculous birth is aimed at us Romans. Maybe it says that Jeshua is a god-emperor like Caesar.'

'So how do they think this anointed one will take power then?' asked Lucius.

'Some Hebrews thought one of the Maccabees who founded Herod's dynasty might have been anointed. He deposed a foreign king a century or so back.'

Lucius frowned in thought for a few moments as he assimilated the strands of the different stories. 'So have I got this right then?' Lucius asked. 'Some think Jeshua is the chosen one and he suddenly turned up in Bethanya yesterday raising the dead. Which would be pretty god-emperor like. So why are they trying to arrest him?'

'Clearly he's still not everybody's choice of "chosen one".' Maximus smiled. 'The priests don't like him. Nor do many of the great and good. He's a nobody. And no one of substance, in Judean eyes at least, comes from Galilee, do they? They think Herod Antipas is a conniving rogue and they may be right about him. He's trying to convince the Hebrews he's anointed too, as his father tried before him.'

Lucius laughed. He had heard about a young Herod Antipas in Rome on an early visit to his backers. Roman nobles, some of whom seemed almost to live in baths, had been anything but complimentary about his odour. Herod's father may have been a legendary water engineer, they had joked, but he obviously hadn't inherited any love of washing with the stuff.

'So the local leaders want Jeshua off the streets then?'

'So it seems. Personally I think there are more troublesome zealots to worry about.' Maximus paused a moment for thought. 'I wonder why is Jonathan worried? Or perhaps it's Joseph Caiaphas himself?' he added, using the High Priest's nickname. 'But then Caiaphas might just be worried about what we'll do if Jeshua stirs up any trouble.'

'Should we be arresting him too? It sounds like he's a zealot.'

'I've not heard that he has direct contact with the brigands. It's people like Barabbas we want. We've plenty to crucify him for. Did Jonathan get Jeshua, by the way, if that was who they were after?'

'They arrested a few, which doesn't sound much like an exercise does it? No names in the report though. Shall I find out if Jeshua was taken?'

'I'd quite like to meet him, if he is in custody,' said Maximus. 'And if he's gone, it would be useful to know that he's coming back before he gets here.'

CHAPTER 10

Jerusalem, the Antonia Fortress dungeons, Friday morning

It was a couple of hours past dawn and the stench in the dungeons under the Antonia Fortress was almost overpowering. Gad had felt dizzy. Anna had retched then held a perfumed cloth to her face as they picked their way through the gloomy cavernous vaults and between their miserable occupants. As he stopped his wife slipping and falling into whatever filth was at their feet, he tried to put purity laws out of his mind.

Gad and his brother, Amos, had been in Bethanya the night before when they had heard the news about Barabbas which was spreading around Jerusalem. A leader of the insurrection, he had been captured near the Dead Sea and was now in the Antonia Fortress with three others taken with him. The news had been greeted glumly in the village: Barabbas was popular and his capture killed any remaining hopes of an imminent end to the Roman occupation of Judea. The Hebrew exile, albeit in the land they believed God had promised them, would continue.

Their son was now three days late and Anna said that a mother's instinct told her that Benjamin was with Barabbas. Gad had tried to convince her that wasn't possible. Why would three merchants from Galilee with a garum shipment

51

end up fighting the Romans? Rumour said that one of the captives was a youth, wounded and unconscious, Anna had pointed out. What if it was Benjamin? Despite being a loyal wife, at one point she had almost shouted at him with agitation.

The men were convinced that Benjamin and his men were delayed somewhere. Benjamin had permission to visit the Essenes at Qumran on the way south to Jerusalem so he was most likely still there. Maybe one of them had become sick, Amos and Gad had speculated. Gad agreed to take Anna to the Antonia Fortress while Amos had stayed at Bethanya that morning to get things ready to leave with Gad for Qumran as soon they got back.

When they had enquired at the main gate of the Antonia Fortress that morning Anna and Gad were not exactly surprised to discover that no one had any information that could help. Gad might now have information of interest to the Romans, he told them. The wounded prisoner was indeed young but the soldier in charge of the gate was a little surprised at Gad: 'Are you sure you want to be associated with a zealot fighter?' he had asked.

'Of course not,' Gad had replied. 'My son isn't a zealot fighter. I know what he really was doing in the Jordan valley. You want to catch the real zealot fighters, don't you? So it will help you if we can identify an innocent so you are not wasting your time, won't it?' Gad had been in the selling business all his life. Now, wherever he was, Benjamin's life might depend on him persuading this soldier to help them at least check he wasn't one of the brigands arrested in the desert.

The soldier had looked at him for a moment and rubbed his face in thought.

'Wait here. I'll get someone to talk to you.' Anna and Gad resigned themselves to a long wait.

'We don't have a name for the wounded prisoner,' a decanus confirmed when he turned up about half an hour later. 'He was badly injured trying to escape and is unconscious. We've got nothing from him. Probably won't either. But if you think you can identify him, follow me.'

When they found Benjamin religious purity suddenly became the least of their worries. According to the decanus, their son had drifted between coma and delirium since he had been arrested and couldn't be interrogated. That and his impending execution put him bottom of everyone's priority list, Gad thought. Nothing had been done to treat his wound except by his fellow prisoners.

Benjamin hadn't recognised their arrival and by torch-light his parents could see his leg was putrifying. Maggots crawled in the livid wound. Anna dissolved into a flood of tears but then, in barely a minute, went from hysteria to lioness: from desperation to a cold conviction that he really knew deep down that she was with him and that she would rescue him.

Anna washed him as best she could amidst the filth and bandaged his leg with cloth that she had brought with her. Now she cradled his head in her lap as she knelt with him. At the same time she spoke to the men captured with him. Benjamin had moaned when Anna had touched the wound: 'He's still with us' one of them nodded encouragingly to her.

The two other captives had been with Barabbas for months. That Sunday morning they had been hiding from the Romans at the top of one of the wadis that ran east from the mountains towards the Dead Sea. They told Gad and Anna that when Benjamin had stumbled across their camp that morning the boy had told them he had been travelling to Jerusalem with a garum shipment. He said he had been attacked by bandits two nights earlier. Both his men had been killed but, being obviously wealthy, Benjamin had been kidnapped. The bandits had taken him south along the Dead Sea but on Saturday night he had escaped while his captors were drunk. He had walked into the mountains that morning hoping to find the road to Jerusalem and found the three of them instead.

The Romans had captured them only a couple of hours later. Had he unwittingly been the cause of their downfall too? Perhaps he had been seen and followed by the Romans? Why he had been startled into running neither knew.

Gad had squatted beside Anna listening to their story while she stroked Benjamin's head. She whispered to him reassuringly. Then Gad stood up and wiped tears from his own eyes. He turned with as much dignity as he could to the decanus who was still with them.

'What will happen now?' Gad asked the decanus. 'Will he be tried for a crime?' The soldier's eyes darted away for a second, then back to Gad.

'The boy's got worse since I last saw him,' he replied evading the question. 'He's pretty quiet now.'

'I am sure you're right about that,' Gad nodded, quickly thinking about how to get this man on their side, 'and thank you very much for helping us find him.' This soldier, ironically another Samaritan, was probably their best chance of keeping their boy alive. If Benjamin lived, of course, he still faced the Roman courts. It was purely bad luck he was here. If Gad could tell Benjamin's story to the authorities he might be released.

'Do you know what he might be charged with?' asked Gad.

'Are you Roman citizens?' asked the Decanus.

'No,' shrugged Gad. 'That would have made a difference, would it?'

'He'd then be tried against written charges. Not being a citizen, he'll be tried verbally. The only witnesses will be the troops who caught him, I suppose.'

'Do you know what the charge will be?' Gad asked.

'No,' he shrugged, slightly evasively.

'Crucifixion?' whispered Gad hoping Anna wouldn't hear.

'I couldn't say,' he replied. Or won't, thought Gad.

'Well thank you for your help. You've been very kind.' He took a small purse from his pocket. 'This is for any expenses you've had until now. Is there a possibility that we could visit him again? Obviously we'll reimburse you for any other expenses.' He raised his eyebrows at the decanus so it was clear how that would work for the decanus himself.

'I'm sure we can arrange something.' The soldier looked at the purse, thought for a moment and then tucked it beneath his tunic. 'You and I will need to speak to the gaoler, of course.'

'Of course,' nodded Gad.

Anna gently put Benjamin's head onto a pile of straw that she had wrapped in a clean cloth to make a pillow. Then she wrung out the cloth she had been using to stroke his head with water from a pail next to her. One of the other prisoners stood as she stood up. He had a son somewhere too, he told her. He gently took the cloth from her and quietly assured her that he would now continue to care for hers.

'Can we bring a physician to treat him too?' asked Anna. She had clearly heard the conversation with the soldier: Gad glanced at the decanus expectantly.

'Ask the gaoler about that too,' nodded the decanus.

PART TWO

TWO WEEKS BEFORE PASSOVER

CHAPTER 11

The Upper City, Jerusalem: Eleazar's house, Sunday evening

Eleazar sipped from a cup of fruit juice as he listened intently to Gad's story about Benjamin's predicament. He was also very interested in Amos' detailed account of their unexpected journey with Jeshua from Jericho the week before. Amos had described their day-long journey through the wilderness of the Wadi Qelt and then their amazement at seeing Lazarus of Bethanya emerge from his tomb that night. Jeshua's miracles were famous but they had never expected to witness one themselves.

Lazarus and his sisters had been horrified when they had heard about Benjamin from Gad and Anna, who had been staying with them while they had searched for him. They agreed also that simple justice suggested that there were grounds to get Benjamin released. Lazarus knew about a young lawyer, one Eleazar, son of Daniel, who was rapidly gaining a reputation as a caring and fearsome advocate. On Sunday morning, following the Sabbath, while Benjamin's parents spent another frustrating day in the Fortress, Lazarus had gone himself to set up this appointment with Eleazar.

Eleazar was even more interested that they had been staying with Lazarus, now the most famous of Jeshua's local friends. Eleazar had also been gripped by their account of the raid on Bethanya. An hour or so before dawn Jeshua had left with a small group of his disciples so the Temple guards must have missed him by a matter of minutes. Amos had no idea where they'd gone but he thought that Jeshua was planning to return for Passover.

Gad had felt annoyed with Amos for being over-detailed. What he saw as his brother's name-dropping had, he decided, started to distract the conversation from the main issue: Benjamin's imminent execution. Eleazar's questions soon moved onto Benjamin's failure to meet them at Gad's agent's shop in a Jerusalem market and their eventual discovery of him, a few days later, in the Antonia Fortress. The days since had, according to Gad, been wasted trying to discover who was responsible for Benjamin's case.

When they had finished Eleazar glanced at his own scribe, who had made notes of the conversation. The scribe nodded at him and Eleazar leaned back on his couch. His eyes closed in thought and he pressed his fingers together in front of his mouth as he turned over the details in his mind. For about a minute there was quiet apart from a last few scratches of stylus on parchment.

'So have you actually discussed your son's case with any of the Romans in the Fortress?' Eleazar asked at last. 'Apart from the soldier that showed you into the dungeon.'

'We tried,' nodded Gad sadly. 'The gaoler was cooperative, once we'd dashed him with some money anyway. But apart from spending the rest of last week waiting in various corridors, we've got nowhere.' Gad looked at his brother, then back to the lawyer and sighed. 'Actually, we still don't really know who we need to see.'

'Did you see anyone?'

'We met some youngster, a Roman officer,' replied Gad. 'Apparently he was in intelligence. We told him what we've told you but nothing happened after that. Nathan, my agent in the city, thinks that there's hope because Barabbas is being kept separately from Benjamin and the other two.'

'Oh, yes?' asked Eleazar enquiringly. 'Why does he think that?'

'If he's being kept separately then he's the one the Romans are talking to, so the Romans may think Benjamin and the others are of little value. If we can show them Benjamin's innocent the Romans may want to release him.'

'I think he may have a point,' nodded Eleazar.

'The quicker the better though,' Gad said emphatically, lest the urgency of his son's predicament was lost. 'Benjamin is in grave danger. He'll be crucified with Barabbas as soon as the Romans think they have heard everything Barabbas has to say. It won't be much comfort if he is saved from being crucified by dying from his wounds.'

Eleazar was quiet again and Amos and Gad looked at the lawyer in the silence. The opulence of this house suggested a man making rapid progress in life. He was clearly still only in his twenties yet this house and its carefully groomed owner told of great wealth. On the other hand Eleazar's home displayed the understatement of those long familiar with wealth. Perhaps money was in his blood? They had seen no evidence of a family which also suggested Eleazar was still a very eligible young man.

Then Eleazar sat forward, as if a course of action had crystallised in his mind: 'From what you have told me I have to agree that your son's situation does indeed look, er,' Eleazar paused for a moment as he selected his next word with care, 'precarious.'

'If he was wandering around lost, then he was simply unlucky to have met Barabbas just before they were all swept up by a Roman patrol. Sadly, even with no direct evidence that Benjamin is a brigand the Romans won't necessarily be sympathetic. You're not Roman citizens, are you? So they're more likely just to go with the obvious. You will have observed that the Romans have been executing a lot of supposedly zealot brigands in recent weeks?' Amos and Gad looked at each other in alarm but said nothing. 'I fear that many were also just innocents in the wrong place at the wrong time.'

'Is there anything you can do?' asked Amos, trying to avoid sounding pleading.

'Well, I say precarious,' Eleazar went on, 'because as we said earlier, he is still alive because the Romans think they might have useful information. So we have some time but probably not much.'

'Firstly I will approach the Roman Governor's office. They will be supervising the framing of any charges. Someone will be keeping a note of things, especially since Barabbas is involved. He is quite popular here, as you've probably gathered, so they'll want justice to be seen to be done.'

'So can you help us then?' asked Gad.

'Well, I can't make any promises but since the Romans probably want to be seen to do everything properly, we might be able to get them to look at Benjamin's case properly too. Barabbas' companions confirmed that your son only joined them in the hours before they were all captured. That's a start.'

'We must get him out of that prison soon,' Gad pointed out insistently. 'When can you see the Governor?'

Eleazar smiled: 'Pilate's not in Jerusalem yet but I'm seeing his staff,' he paused and looked questioningly at his scribe, 'tomorrow, I think?' The assistant nodded a confirmation, 'I'll request a review of the case then. I also know someone with a personal connection with the

Governor. I will also write and ask him to contact the Governor directly. You're still staying with Lazarus at Bethanya?'

'Yes,' confirmed Gad. 'We visit Benjamin every day too. That's where my wife is now. Shall we come back tomorrow?'

'I'll leave those details with Reuben here. He will contact you when there is any news.' Eleazar rose. 'Gentlemen, I will do everything I can to help your son. But please don't expect a miracle,' he smiled. 'I am not Rabbi Jeshua, after all.' He gave a faint nod of his head. 'If you will excuse me.' The others stood as Eleazar left the room.

CHAPTER 12

Jerusalem, the High Priest's office, the Temple, Monday morning

'Eleazar!' said Annas, as Eleazar was shown into the High Priest's quarters overlooking the Temple Courts. He and Jonathan were sitting on couches but rose as he was shown into the room by a slave. 'Your message said you had news of Jeshua of Nazareth, so I asked Jonathan to join us.'

'Good. I hoped that you would,' said Eleazar. The lawyer greeted both with a kiss on each cheek and the three men sat down. Annas was at the head of the table, Jonathan and Eleazar each side.

'I had a very interesting meeting yesterday evening. There are a number of threads all connected to the matters we discussed at dinner last week. Can we keep this private for now?'

Annas beckoned to the slave to leave and a scribe who was working in the office behind them looked up and nodded that he had taken the hint. The scribe closed the door behind him and they were alone.

'As you know,' Eleazar began, 'Barabbas was arrested last week and is being interrogated in the Antonia with three of his men. Yesterday Lazarus of Bethany called at my house to request I meet with a guest of his whose son, it transpires, is the injured youth no one could identify.' He paused, noting with satisfaction that both Annas and Jonathan both leaned forward with interest.

'The father is a garum merchant from Tiberias in Galilee. He arrived with his wife in Jerusalem last week to meet his son, having travelled from Jericho in the company, would you believe it, of Jeshua of Nazareth.'

'Never!' said Annas, smiling at Jonathan, who shook his head in disbelief. 'That could be a stroke of good fortune. Where are they all now?'

'Staying with Lazarus. As we thought, Jeshua suspected you would try to arrest him and left Bethanya. But only about an hour before your men got there. They believe that Jeshua will return for the Passover festival but have no idea where he is now. Apparently one of Jeshua's disciples knew somewhere in the wilderness but they didn't tell anyone in Bethanya where.' Eleazar sat back nonchalantly and looked at Annas.

'I can't believe it,' smiled Jonathan. 'We've been trying to find someone who can lead us to Jeshua and a contact falls right into our lap. So where have you left things, Eleazar?'

'Obviously I will do my best for the boy. He'd actually been kidnapped by bandits a couple of days earlier, his shipment stolen and two of his father's men killed.'

'Others in Barabbas's band perhaps?' wondered Jonathan.

'They could indeed have been zealots trying to raise money to fund operations against the Romans,' nodded Eleazar. 'Who knows? Anyway, he managed to escape and was trying to get to Jerusalem. He stumbled across Barabbas and the other two just before the Romans captured them all on Sunday morning. I'll help the others too, of course. When I checked last night the Romans refused to let me see Barabbas. I fear he'll be having a very bad time.'

'Yes, I can imagine,' said Annas sadly, disgusted at the

thought of the torture that Barabbas was probably suffering. 'Barabbas isn't such a bad man, actually. I think I knew his father. Died when the boy was young, if it's the man I'm thinking of. If so, the old man was a fiery one too. Do you know about the others?'

'The other two used to be farmers somewhere in the north. They were out of their depth in debt. Nothing unusual; there's lots in the zealot bands like that. Their land, wives and children were all sold to pay the debts but it wasn't enough. Given a choice between slavery themselves or a life with the zealots they ended up fighting with Barabbas.' The men were silent for a moment.

'Sad, but nothing else we can do for them,' said Annas finally.

Jonathan had been deep in thought about what Eleazar had said. 'Did your clients give any indication of when Jeshua was returning?' he asked.

'No,' replied Eleazar. 'The boy's uncle was quite talkative but I don't think anyone knows when. Probably because Jeshua knows you want to arrest him and hasn't told anyone.'

'Well its not the news we wanted,' said Annas, 'but at least we know he is coming back here so we don't need to scatter people all over the country. What are your thoughts, Jonathan?'

'He has the element of surprise and with more pilgrims arriving every day its going to be hard to find him in the crowds. Did your people say what he looks like?'

'No, but I have seen him myself when he was in Jerusalem before. I would probably recognise him if I saw him but he doesn't exactly stand out in a crowd. In fact there is nothing special about his appearance at all. He just looked like a Hebrew man aged about thirty.'

'There's plenty of those here,' Jonathan frowned.

'Jonathan, How many men would it take to watch all the roads?' asked Annas.

'Day and night, just on the major routes?' Jonathan did some mental arithmetic for a few moments. 'About forty. I doubt we can sustain that for more than a week or so either. And Jeshua can travel across country. There are already pilgrims camping out in the hills around the city. It'll be easy for him to slip past us and it'll get easier as more pilgrims arrive.'

'Joseph won't be too impressed if we pull forty of his guards away,' said Annas, shaking his head. 'especially as the festival gets closer. If we don't even know what Jeshua looks like I'm not sure there's any point in trying to spot him coming.'

'I agree,' said Jonathan, slightly relieved since he shared that view. 'But can we use these people in Bethanya?'

'Can I help?' asked Eleazar.

'Well, yes, you could. Could one of your people point out the parents?' said Jonathan. 'Then I'll get one of mine to befriend them and keep a watch through them.'

'When I've met Pilate's people this afternoon, I'll have one of my assistants go to Bethanya to update the family,' said Eleazar. 'Have your man go with him.'

CHAPTER 13

Nicodemus' estate, west of Jerusalem, Friday evening

In the warm spring evening Pilate and Nicodemus were enjoying a pre-dinner walk through one of the several gardens on Nicodemus' estate near Jerusalem. They had already spent the afternoon discussing different business matters. Such meetings suited both sides. Nicodemus advised Pilate on how the Judeans might feel about his plans and, in return, Pilate listen to representations from Nicodemus. Pilate's guards shadowed them discreetly but on Pilate's instructions they were out of hearing. Nicodemus, elderly and rotund, was hardly a threat.

Their relationship encompassed pragmatism and respect. It had started during Pilate's early years through a business project to supply water to pilgrims visiting Jerusalem. Though brittle at the start, respect had grown and, to some extent, become friendship. Nicodemus had vast wealth, enough to require good economic order to maintain it. Pilate sometimes reflected that knowing Nicodemus might have helped him avoid the earlier humiliation over the standards displayed in the Antonia Fortress.

'It's interesting that you say that Jeshua isn't of this world,' Nicodemus smiled. 'From what he's told me, he is seeking to build a completely different kind of kingdom. That's one reason why he never talks about himself as king. Or even *messiah*, which has a kingly resonance in Hebrew ears. He is not just avoiding sedition either. Jeshua avoids calling himself a king to discourage anyone from trying to make him one. A crowd did try once, you know.'

'I didn't hear about that,' said Pilate, slightly puzzled.

'It was some hotheads in Galilee,' went on Nicodemus. 'Jeshua did one of his vanishing tricks so nothing happened. Funnily enough his occasional disappearances seem to get people as excited as his appearances.'

'He can vanish at will?' asked Pilate, incredulously.

'So some have said,' Nicodemus laughed. 'I've never seen it myself. I suspect people get so fired up they just don't notice Jeshua discreetly heading off in the other direction. You know how uncaught fish sometimes grow in the telling. We Hebrews can be quite fiery, you know. "Israel" means "He who argues with God."'

'So I gather. Pity Jeshua's too busy to meet me,' said Pilate, with the air of the one not invited to a party.

'I'm sure he'll be delighted to meet you. Would you like me to arrange it?' enquired Nicodemus in a helpful tone.

'Thank you,' replied Pilate, a trace of genuine enthusiasm in his voice. 'Yes, one day that would be nice but for now I need to decide how dangerous he might be and what I should do about him.'

'Why do you think he might be dangerous?' asked Nicodemus.

Pilate grimaced and scratched his head. 'I'm worried that I have no way to deter him if he threatens law and order. That manifesto he proclaimed at Nazareth[16] for instance. Love your enemies? Pray for your persecutors? That really is in another world. We can't govern like that, can we?'

'One does wonder how politics and economics would operate in his world,' Nicodemus acknowledged. 'But we Hebrews are no strangers to God sending us prophets telling us things like this. Centuries ago we were told to trust God in the face of military power.'

'Oh? So what happened then?' asked Pilate.

'We naturally trusted in diplomacy backed by force of arms instead. Then we were taken into exile by the Assyrians. The Lord Almighty clearly has a sense of irony.'

'Sorry. Yes, I remember you telling me about the exile.'

'Perhaps the prophets were right,' Nicodemus mused. 'There is something compelling about Jeshua's vision of a world in which God's will can be done on earth. You Romans are enthralled with the Greeks' and their division of the cosmos into material and spiritual realms. None of the Roman or Greek god's really care about what happens to us on earth, do they?'

'That's an understatement,' Pilate chuckled in acknowledgement.

'Jeshua is a Hebrew though. We Hebrews see heaven and earth alongside each other in some mysterious sense,' Nicodemus continued. 'What you do here makes a difference in heaven and vice versa, strange though that may sound to a Roman or a Greek.'

'So is Jeshua just suggesting a new way of living then?' asked Pilate.

'Well, Jeshua hasn't written any new laws. Instead he focuses on the impact of our existing laws. Lawyers like me are good at recommending we just follow laws obediently. Jeshua makes us look at things in the light of those laws and then asks us to work out how God would have us behave. "God's will be done on earth as it is in heaven[17]" is a prayer he teaches his followers.

A meal had been laid out in the garden and they sat on

either side of a dining table underneath a large awning slung between four trees that stood at each corner of a paved square, some twenty yards on each side. Smaller ornamental shrubs and flowers were planted along each side. Pilate accepted a glass of wine and savoured it while a slave served the food. As the slaves retired to await further summons Pilate looked back at Nicodemus.

'But surely God's will being done on earth is *all* about lawmakers like you?' Pilate asked. 'And law enforcers like me, for that matter.' Nicodemus looked at Pilate and thought about that.

'If he were here I think Jeshua might tell you a story,' Nicodemus said eventually. 'One of his famous stories is about a farmer who sowed seed in a plot alongside a road[18]. The seed was all the same but the soil varied a lot. There were bits of rocky path, thin soil and thistle patches as well as the good soil. Obviously where it fell into good soil the seeds grew well. Now, the fertilizer that is dug from beside the Dead Sea is marvellous for improving soil. He often refers to his people as the fertilizer of the earth. By being mixed into the world, just like fertilizer into poor soil, they improve it, so the world works better. Just being in the world, and acting as if we take God's will seriously, God's will is done more than it would otherwise be. I think that's how Jeshua would say that God's Kingdom is going to come here on earth.'

'But if that is Hebrew thinking why does he seem to upset your people even more than he upsets mine?' Pilate asked, laughing.

CHAPTER 14

'Well, sometimes that's the mystery of it,' Nicodemus also laughed gently. 'Jeshua and, for instance, the Pharisees are actually quite close, just because they all care passionately about many of the same things. Families are often argumentative because people do care and we Jews often feel like a family. They say the easiest way to find a rabbi school is just by following the sound of the shouting. It annoys some of my Pharisee friends that Jeshua seems to be radically reinterpreting our laws.' Nicodemus sipped some wine. 'Actually some would say he's ignoring them.'

'And ignoring the law is surely where he could be dangerous,' said Pilate, more seriously. 'With all due respect to the High Priest, I'm not that worried if he offends the religious. But what if he starts breaking Roman laws? Especially if half the population of Jerusalem are cheering him on.' He drained his glass, put it down and sat back, scratching his chin in frustration.

'Prefect, don't make the same mistake many of my fellow Jews make. Herod, the Tetrarch, for instance, is crazy with worry. But Jeshua is not going to become a political leader as we would know it, although he is firmly in the real world.'

'Has Herod Antipas got a problem with Jeshua too? I thought it was the Baptist that upset him?'

'Yes, Herod was annoyed when John objected to

Herod's relationship with his brother's estranged wife, Herodias. She then had Herod execute John[19]. Herod wants to be the King of the Jews, like his father. He fears Jeshua threatens him.

'But you say Jeshua doesn't share that ambition?' asked Pilate.

'I don't think so, though even the Baptist probably thought that Jeshua was the ancient prophet Elijah too. In scripture, Elijah famously brought fire down from heaven onto pagan heads. Did you know that Jeshua and John were cousins? I think John was also hoping his cousin would bring fire down onto Herod, you Romans and our own sinners.'

'I thought Jeshua heals people?'

'He does heal people,' nodded Nicodemus. 'But since we often expect to condemn sick people as sinners, healing them sends a very different message. How many respectable men spend time with the disreputable? John was very confused. Just before he died he asked Jeshua whether he really was the anointed one or whether we should all look for another *messiah*[20].'

'So Jeshua isn't the *messiah* most Jews expect?'

'Well, If I've understood Jeshua, we may be misunderstanding what the Lord Almighty is about. Jeshua sometimes seems to say that some religious folk are as sinful as the sinners we shun. So he criticises many who are just blindly following rules.'

'Really?' asked Pilate, intrigued by this completely alien train of thought. He glanced up and nodded at a slave who was offering to fill his glass again.

'Jeshua tells another story about a man who was attacked by robbers and left for dead on the road to Jericho[21]. A Jewish scribe and then a priest come past him heading to Jerusalem and refuse to go near him. Of course, every Jew would know they were probably going to the Temple for worship.'

'Presumably they wouldn't touch him in case he was dead?' asked Pilate.

'Precisely,' nodded Nicodemus. 'If they touched a dead body, they would be unclean when they got to the Temple so they wouldn't be able to carry out their duties. Jeshua, I think, is suggesting that we might abandon such rules at that point.'

'Oh I see,' nodded Pilate. 'Not helping the man would offend God much more than becoming ritually unclean.'

'That's exactly what Jeshua's story might suggest,' Nicodemus agreed.

'Perhaps it served the man right for travelling alone on the road to Jericho,' observed Pilate with a smile, 'especially if he went through the Wadi Qelt.'

'Well, indeed so,' Nicodemus said. 'I think that's the valley that the psalmist who wrote "though I walk through the valley of the shadow of death[22]" had in mind. Are you familiar with the psalms?' Pilate nodded. He knew about that one at least.

'What upsets my more literal-minded Pharisee friends even more,' Nicodemus continued, 'is that the hero of the story, who rescues the traveller, is a Samaritan. If Jeshua is scorning our ritual purity he also undermines our sense of racial purity too. Might God approve more of a Samaritan who ignores God's law than a Hebrew who obeys it?

'So why don't stories like that upset you?' Pilate took a mouthful of food and looked at Nicodemus expectantly.

'Perhaps I'm a pragmatist, or just getting gentler with age,' Nicodemus smiled. 'I think Jeshua is saying something quite important too. My faith tells me I am already a member of the people of God.'

'I struggle with any faith that doesn't seem to believe in

gods, plural, but you know that of us.' Pilate sipped his wine and listened intently.

'Jeshua teaches that we are all God's creatures, so God loves us already. He then invites us to act like it more often. Many of my friends would never entertain a gentile but, since God is the God of the whole cosmos, I feel I serve God better by being hospitable, to you for instance. I know it's pragmatic for both of us to be discreet about meetings like this though.' Nicodemus chuckled and added, 'Actually Jeshua sometimes jokes that I'd rather not be seen with him either.'

'So would he agree that only fools blindly obey rules?' smiled Pilate.

'Perhaps,' Nicodemus looked at Pilate mischievously. 'Clearly Jeshua wouldn't heal a gentile if he didn't think God loves gentiles, too.'

'I struggle with the thought that any god loves me,' Pilate observed quietly. 'Or, frankly, even that any god loves anything, of this world at least.'

'Really? Why?' asked Nicodemus, leaning forward with interest.

'The gods,' Pilate smiled at Nicodemus, 'well Rome's gods, at least, don't seem interested in any of us. Oh, they challenge us to prove ourselves. Those who make the grade might become immortal like them. But do gods really care? They struggle with each other, certainly. They try to dominate each other. And us mortals.' Pilate paused and Nicodemus saw a faint look of sadness come into Pilate's eyes.

'Look at gods and sex for instance,' Pilate went on. 'I've seen soldiers rape women after battles. That's certainly not love. It's not even proper sex. Rape is a violent expression of domination. It's about hurting and degrading someone because one needs to feel dominant. The gods don't make *love* very often. They aren't careful or gentle. Normally they just copulate like animals. Not even for enjoyment much of the time. Just for power and position.' Pilate rolled the wine around in his glass, studying the colour absently. He paused, reflecting on loves and losses.

'So what sorts of gods are those?' asked Nicodemus quietly. Pilate looked at him and back to his wine. He shrugged with a smile and answered:

'The Stoics, I think, teach that we are all already 'gods': that we control ourselves within our own inner world. Mostly I feel life is just a struggle to survive and to get on. Gods are for the upper classes,' Pilate laughed ironically, 'especially the ones I don't belong to. The ones who can afford to copulate like cattle too, just for power and perhaps to enthral the lower classes. Are upper and lower orders united by a common sense of immorality, I wonder?'

Nicodemus laughed, enjoying that thought. He hadn't seen a philosophical side to the Prefect before. 'You should read some psalms. They're in Greek too, if you don't read Hebrew. Many psalmists and songwriters struggle with the same thoughts.'

'Is that because writers and singers are natural whiners?' Pilate asked.

Nicodemus laughed again but paused as a thought struck him: 'Jeshua would understand how you feel. You really should meet him. He's not a knight like you. He's just the son of a builder. And from Galilee too! You know about our "Galilean" jokes, don't you?'

'Yes I've heard a few,' acknowledged Pilate with a smile. 'But knowing that Jeshua would understand how I feel doesn't help much, even if he makes a lot of sense, even if he's quite reasonable. He just doesn't fit in. Replacing the obedience that gets things rubbing along with freedom to ignore the rules could be very dangerous.'

'Perhaps,' acknowledged Nicodemus. 'My Pharisee friends would agree with you certainly. The Sadducees too for that matter. They get very angry when Jeshua undermines their authority, the more so since they know the common people feel he's got more authority than them.'

'Exactly,' said Pilate, emphatically. 'That's why government cannot cherish rebels. People like him just point out absurdity and fault. People with power may not be perfect but if we are mocked we cannot govern. Government knows what's best for the people and, for all our faults, without us the people would be worse off, wouldn't they?'

PART THREE

THE LAST WEEK BEFORE PASSOVER

CHAPTER 15

Jerusalem, the Antonia Fortress, Sunday afternoon

It was late on Sunday afternoon and Maximus was discussing deployments for the week ahead with some of his subordinates. As they talked he became increasingly aware of raised voices elsewhere in the Antonia Fortress. Then Lucius appeared in the doorway in full battle dress. Maximus looked, slightly crossly, across the maps and models that he was using to explain his orders to his men.

'Problem?' Maximus asked, allowing a trace of annoyance to remain in his voice.

'Bit of a drama, yes,' replied Lucius, with the assurance of one who knew Maximus would want to know the news he could share. 'There's a huge crowd of Hebrew pilgrims heading from the Mount of Olives towards the eastern gate. The reaction force is deploying in case of trouble. Apparently Jeshua of Nazareth is leading the procession.'

Maximus thought for a few moments then said to his men: 'Thank you, gentlemen, I am sorry but I do need to respond to this. We'll continue two hours from now if there are no other orders. In the meantime get your men ready to move, please.' He looked back at Lucius: 'Wait there, I'll be with you in a minute.' Maximus called for his slave and moved to the stand where his breastplate, helmet and sword were hung as his men left. Once dressed and armed he strode out of the office.

'So what's the story, Cornelius?' he asked as they descended to the fortress gate.

'I was on the east wall above the gate when pilgrims started gathering on the top of the Mount of Olives around someone on a donkey. As he headed down the hill towards the city there was lots of cheering. Hundreds of people from all those pilgrim camps that are all over the hills took off their cloaks and tore fronds off the trees. They were putting them on the path in front of him for the donkey to walk on. People were cheering him on as he came through the gate, presumably to go to the Temple.'

'What did you do next?' asked Maximus.

'I came back here and there was a section leaving to back up the eastern gate. Some of the Hebrews were shouting at them. Mainly in Aramaic but I still picked out "Hosanna" and "Jeshua". Is this another uprising, then?'

'Well it could be an exciting end to the day,' acknowledged Maximus.

Twenty soldiers had fallen into two ranks in the courtyard. Maximus told the decanus in command that he and Lucius would follow them to the Temple. The latest news was that a large but peaceful crowd was heading into the Temple. The decanus' orders were to report to the Duty Centurion, who had already left with instructions to "stiffen the resolve" of the Captain of the Temple Guards, a phrase delivered to Maximus with a wry smile by the decanus. Maximus and Lucius followed the soldiers onto the streets.

The Antonia Fortress was situated at the north-west corner of the Temple Mount. If they intended to go to the Temple the least inflammatory way was from the Antonia on the north-western corner of the Temple Mount and down to the southern gates. The Romans marched along a pavement on the western side of the Mount lined with traders' booths. The crowds parted as the soldiers shouted at people and barged their way through.

Fifteen minutes brought them to the south-west corner of the Mount and past some of the booths where traders sold animals for sacrifice. The bleating and the smell of animal waste suggested that trade was already brisk, especially among the lambs to be sacrificed and eaten at Passover in a few days. The crowd, however, seemed distracted. Many people stood around, chatting excitedly. They seemed unclear about what might happen next.

The Roman troops ploughed a way up the southern Temple steps through lines of pilgrims queuing to use the ritual baths. These were located just outside the Temple Courts. Pilgrims would wash ceremonially before entering the Temple to perform sacrifices. At the top of the steps the troops halted. Although the Court of the Gentiles immediately inside was, as the name suggested, open to non-Hebrews, it would have been unnecessarily provocative to march into the Temple as a formed body of troops.

CHAPTER 16

Jerusalem, the Temple Courts, Sunday afternoon

The Jewish guards on the entrances to the Temple precincts said that the Duty Centurion was already inside. The two Roman officers, accompanied by the decanus and four soldiers followed the guards' directions. The atmosphere was tense and a hush had descended on people who, having purified themselves, were now waiting to enter the Temple itself. Apart from a low buzz of conversation, most of the noise was from the animals, doubtless disorientated by their ordeal so far. Maximus wondered momentarily if they had any sense of their forthcoming death and butchery.

Maximus saw his fellow centurion standing with Jonathan in the shade of a colonnade looking into the Court of the Gentiles. Maximus tapped him on the shoulder. Both he and Jonathan turned around and Maximus briefly indicated the presence of Lucius and the commander of the reinforcements. There were nodded acknowledgements then they turned back to the object of everyone's attention.

About twenty yards away was a man in a shabby mantle[23]. He seemed to be admiring the buildings and seemed not to have seen that he had halted business in this part of the Temple, nor that everyone was looking at him. A group of equally shabby men and women kept switching their attention between the crowd and the man, who could have been leading them on a tour. Though obviously Hebrew, their country clothes contrasted with the urbane style of the locals. Maximus guessed they were Galileans. Jonathan, from a wealthy Judean family himself, had once jibed to Maximus that Galileans were "very nice people; such a pity they make their own clothes." Maximus could see what Jonathan had meant.

Suddenly it struck Maximus that this was Jeshua of Nazareth. Some of his disciples at least could see the stir they were causing. One moment they would pay attention to Jeshua. The next some nervously looked at the crowd who were in turn studying them intently. Several looked quite mature, in their thirties perhaps, others seemed hardly more than youths.

They were both men and women too. He had heard that Jeshua scandalised some by allowing women among his disciples. It was debatable which was more offensive: the single women or the married ones. Maximus wondered about their husbands. Dead already perhaps? Even if a woman had the courage, or temerity perhaps, to leave husband or father, Maximus wasn't surprised that she might be nervous being the centre of such attention. The young men seemed to feel the same.

Maximus studied the Hebrew faces around Jonathan. Several were priests and scribes, some clearly on duty. Behind them in the wider crowd were many of the religious sorts normally found in the Temple. There were hundreds of pilgrims, clearly of all social classes. Alongside well-dressed merchants were shabby labourers. Outside the Temple, hundreds more were being held back by the Temple guards at the entrances. Other variations of dress indicated foreigners, doubtless members of the Hebrew *diaspora,* in Jerusalem for the festival.

Jeshua had been standing with his back to them, looking at the Temple itself, perhaps the biggest building that many of Jeshua's band would ever see. Smoke from sacrifices was curling away into the blue sky.

Suddenly Jeshua turned and looked straight at Jonathan and the party of Roman soldiers of which Maximus was a part. Then he strode across the courtyard towards them and Jonathan jerked in shock: he hadn't expected a personal encounter. Before he had could react Jeshua reached him and looked him in the eye:

'Excuse me, please may we pass by?' Jeshua asked with a polite smile. Did Jeshua know he was addressing those with the greatest authority in the crowd? This must be deliberate, thought Maximus. He smiled inwardly at the sheer nerve of one who, apart from a gleam of confidence in his eye, looked like the humblest of the humble. Jonathan moved aside without thinking. There was a ripple of laughter from the less respectable elements in the crowd at the sight of the Captain of the Temple Guard, in all his finery, meekly making way for a shabby peasant. Jonathan blushed with embarrassment but said nothing.

Jeshua calmly thanked him and led his band past them. As he did so, Maximus briefly caught Jeshua's eye. The crowd behind them parted and, as the last of the disciples passed him Maximus found he was grinning too.

Jeshua's band passed under the colonnade and out of the Temple precincts through the nearby gate. As they left there was a renewed buzz of conversation.

CHAPTER 17

Jerusalem, Pilate's office in the Palace of Herod, Sunday evening

Maximus saluted as he entered Pilate's private office a couple of hours later. 'Welcome back, Prefect. I hope you won't find Jerusalem too trying after the delights of the coast.'

As young officer and junior legionary they had soldiered together in Germany and, now reunited in Judea, they had found an easy warmth of old familiarity.

'Centurion! Good evening,' smiled Pilate lightly. 'Good to see you again too. I'm hoping the intrigue here will make up for the lack of gentle sea-breezes.' Pilate leaned forward over the desk at which he was seated. He had finished his work for the day. He put both elbows on the desk, entwined his fingers, leaned his chin on his hands and looked at his assistant. The man had put most of the papers they'd been working on, already rolled up, into a bag that hung over his shoulder. Then having bowed to the Prefect he turned to leave, smiling at the Centurion as he departed by the door through which Maximus had just entered.

'I hear it's been an exciting afternoon at the Temple,' said Pilate.

'Jeshua, the rabbi from Nazareth, was showing some of his disciples around,' replied Maximus. 'But arriving on a donkey through the eastern gate caused some excitement. As you know, Sir, that's how the Jewish "anointed one" is expected to arrive.'

'Indeed I do. Can we expect trouble then?' asked Pilate, his eyes suggesting to Maximus that his superior was genuinely concerned. Maximus thought before he answered. Jeshua's band had seemed oblivious to the excitement they'd caused. They'd also seemed the last kind of people to threaten trouble.

'Nothing I saw there today suggested they would cause us any trouble, Sir. There's no intelligence suggesting Jeshua has any means to attack us either.'

'Good, but we'll be wise to keep an eye out for trouble. He may mean no harm but there's no telling what the mob around him might do.'

'That's our assessment too, Sir,' Maximus nodded, hinting that the garrison had already organised itself with that in mind. 'Was that why you wanted to see me?'

'No,' replied Pilate, 'something completely different actually. You picked up Barabbas and his band, didn't you? A good piece of work, incidentally. Well done.'

'Thank you, Sir,' Maximus smiled.

'I've had representations about one of them.' Pilate tapped one of two scrolls in front of him. 'There was a youth taken with him, another Galilean funnily enough but from Tiberias. He was quite badly wounded too.' Pilate looked up. 'Is that right?'

'One of them made a run for it when we caught them,' replied Maximus. 'He was stopped and, yes, he was quite badly hurt. I don't think he ever gave us his name. I think he's been either unconscious or delirious ever since.'

Pilate looked back at the papers. 'Apparently he was attacked by, and then escaped from, brigands who supposedly killed his father's men. Father is a reputable merchant from Tiberias, the boy works for him and was travelling with a shipment of his goods.' Pilate looked up. 'Rather good garum, I am told.' He looked back to the document. 'They claim he found Barabbas just before you did and was simply unfortunate to be taken with him. I am told that he is innocent of any charges that we might make.' Pilate looked up at Maximus expectantly. 'Any comments?'

'I can only tell you what I saw, Prefect,' replied Maximus, after a pause for thought. 'We spotted Barabbas and his men camped at the top of a stream so we cordoned off the area and arrested them. No one went in or out of the camp in the hour it took us to set the cordon. They didn't see us surround them. The boy ran into soldiers who had been placed precisely to stop anyone escaping.'

'Do you think he is a brigand as well?' asked Pilate.

'Not necessarily. All I know for certain is that he was with Barabbas. Do you want to release the boy?'

'If he's innocent, of course I do. This is all from a local lawyer called Eleazar. He says Barabbas and the others can confirm that the boy arrived at their camp just before you did. Do you know Eleazar?'

'By reputation,' nodded Maximus. 'He's young and upcoming.'

'Indeed?' Pilate paused, then tapped the other scroll on his desk. 'I also have this from a Sanhedrin member, who has also asked me to release the boy unless there is direct evidence against him. His parents are apparently in Jerusalem. The boy was on a trip for his father and the shipment and his companions are missing. I know Nicodemus well. He wouldn't put his name to anything like this if he didn't believe it to be the truth. Would you agree?'

'I'm sure you're right, Sir. One thought, if you will

permit?' Pilate raised an eyebrow. 'Barabbas' companions are of no real military significance. If one happens to be entirely innocent, so be it.'

'That's my view too,' Pilate agreed. 'Would you investigate, please?

CHAPTER 18

Jerusalem, the Antonia Fortress, Monday morning

As the second of the prisoners was escorted out of Maximus' office and back to the dungeon, Maximus stood up, stretched, then went to a table where his slave had placed a jug of water. He filled a beaker and drank looking out of the window across Jerusalem. There was a knock at the door.

'Come in', he called. The gaoler entered, accompanied by the decanus whose men had been escorting the prisoners.

'Centurion,' said the decanus as he saluted. 'You asked about the parents of that boy from Tiberias? While you were questioning the two who were with Barabbas, the parents arrived with his uncle. I've got them outside if you want to talk to them. In fact they're keen to talk to you.'

'They're here now? Good! Well done. Show them in.' Maximus took his place behind his desk and waited. Gad, Anna and Amos were shown into the office and stood in front of his desk.

'You're the parents of Benjamin, the boy from Tiberias?' asked Maximus.

'Yes, we are, Sir.' said Gad. 'Thank you very much for seeing us. I know Benjamin was captured with this Barabbas fellow but Benjamin has had no part in the insurrection. We've been trying to find someone in authority to talk to for days so we can confirm his innocence. He was just in the wrong place at the wrong time.' Maximus could see Gad's relief at finally talking to someone in charge. He raised a hand to cut him off.

'Since when, exactly, have you been seeking someone in authority?'

Gad thought for a moment. 'Well, we got to Jerusalem to meet Benjamin at the Temple two Sundays ago. We found him here in the fortress at the end of that week.' He looked at Amos who nodded his agreement. 'We've been here every day since. I'm sorry we didn't know to ask for you. If we had known we would have come straight to you. We saw a lawyer last week. He raised the matter with the Governor.'

'Yes, I know about the lawyer,' nodded Maximus. If he had known these people had been here, he could have raised the matter with Pilate, rather than being summoned by him. He would have words with a few people. 'How is the boy, by the way?'

'Oh, better, thank you, Sir,' said Gad, smiling at the thought Maximus might actually care. 'He's weak but he regained consciousness yesterday. Even his leg seems to be healing at last.'

'Good. So when you arrived in Jerusalem last Sunday where were you expecting to meet him?'

'We had planned to meet at my agent's place in one of the markets. Benjamin and two of my men were bringing in a shipment of garum sauce. We make it by the Sea of Galilee. We regularly bring shipments to Jerusalem. Benjamin is just starting to work in the business. It was his first journey in charge of a shipment.'

'How do you normally get here?'

'Normally we go along the coastal route to avoid Samaria but I had allowed Benjamin to go along the Jordan Valley so he could visit Qumran on the way. Until last night we only knew what his cell mates told us. Benjamin told us last night that bandits killed our men, stole the shipment and kidnapped him. He managed to escape at night and was trying to find a route to Jerusalem. The next morning he found Barabbas instead, just before your soldiers arrived.'

'So why did he run?' asked Maximus.

'He thought you were the kidnappers still chasing him,' replied Gad. 'He thought he would be killed if they took him again. When the horn sounded he wondered if Barabbas and his men were part of the same band and just made a snap decision not to stay to find out. He only saw you were soldiers when one ran him through with a spear. He knows he made the wrong decision. If he'd known you were soldiers he'd have been delighted to see you. Apart from lots of pain, he can't remember much until he woke up yesterday. Are you investigating his case? Is there anything else we can tell you that might help?'

Maximus looked at them and thought for a few moments. These people wanted to tell their story, he thought, which suggests it was probably true. Maximus had just pointed out to Benjamin's cell-mates that the boy's fate would have no influence on their own so their best chance was to tell the truth. He had got the same story from both of them.

'No, not for now. I would like you to stay here in the Fortress while I am examining the case. The decanus here will arrange somewhere for you to wait.' He looked at the decanus who nodded his acknowledgment and added a crisp 'Sir!'

'Of course, Sir,' Gad assured him. Maximus noted the relief in his voice. 'May my wife see Benjamin while we're waiting?'

'Sorry, no, not yet,' replied Maximus. 'I may need to speak to him and I don't want you seeing him again until I have done that. Just stay in the fortress, please.' Then he softened his tone. 'Don't worry. I don't think it will take too much longer.'

'Thank you, Sir. I'm sorry if we can't add much more to the story, but this'll demonstrate that I am a garum merchant at least,' Gad produced a small bottle from a bag hung over his shoulder and smiled at Maximus. 'Please accept it.'

Maximus, like most Romans, enjoyed garum and smiled at the thought. 'Well, shall we say that I will take it as confirmation of your occupation. I think I'd prefer you to keep it, though, at least until I've resolved the matter. Go with the decanus and I'll send for you when I need to see you again.'

'As you wish, Sir,' smiled Gad. Amos and Anna followed his lead and bowed before they were shown out.

When they'd gone Maximus scratched his head in thought. It was a simple enough story and everyone seemed genuine. So where might there be a more sinister explanation? Or am I just being too suspicious? he wondered. If there was some serious plot to release a prisoner why was it this boy and not Barabbas himself? He also doubted that someone like Nicodemus would perjure himself.

Most importantly at the moment he was also cross that these people had sat around in the Fortress for over a week without someone mentioning it to him. Someone in our system is pretty slack, he thought, but then he'd been a soldier long enough to write a guide to organisational incompetence.

Let's see what Barabbas has to say for himself, he thought as he called for the decanus.

CHAPTER 19

Maximus remembered the fanatical stare in Barabbas' eyes from their meeting in the desert. He was still dressed in the same clothes and Maximus could tell, from the smell, that they really needed a wash. Fresh injuries suggested that the interrogators had not been particularly gentle with him.

'You remember who I am?' asked Maximus.

Barabbas looked at him and said nothing. He's obviously learned somewhere that the secret to being interrogated is to say nothing beyond one's name, thought Maximus. He probably assumes I'm a new approach and he's done well if he's managed to say nothing but his name for two weeks.

'You're a bit in the shit, aren't you?' Maximus observed. 'What did you all think you'd achieve by fighting us?'

'This is our land. The Lord gave it to us. The Lord will deliver us,' said Barabbas flatly.

'You see dying on a cross as delivery?' asked Maximus, noticing the monotonous reply. Maybe he's been more talkative with the interrogators after all, he thought.

'Lots of my people have died, some terribly. The Lord vindicated them and will vindicate us.'

'By you all fighting us? Even if you'd beaten our auxiliaries, do you know when a Roman legion last lost a fight?' Barabbas said nothing to that.

'Exactly,' smiled Maximus. 'We're rather good at dealing with violent rebels, as you now know.'

'There'll be more of us.'

'Doubtless, but violence plays to our strengths, doesn't it?'

'The Lord of Israel will overcome you,' Barabbas said, flatly. 'Just as he overcame the last heathens and gave us back our land.'

'A long time ago,' nodded Maximus, 'and with our help. What do you think of Jeshua, from Galilee? You might have heard that he arrived here yesterday. You probably heard him. And that he entered the Temple riding on a donkey. Isn't he coming to restore Israel too?'

'They say Jeshua's approach to you Romans is that I pray for you and carry your bags for an extra mile more than you tell me to[24]. If I do that will you leave my country?' asked Barabbas.

'Probably not,' replied Maximus.

'Sounds like Jeshua might not be getting our land back either then, doesn't it?'

'So you don't think his non-violent approach will make much difference?'

'He upsets my people more than he does yours,' Barabbas laughed sarcastically. 'Here and in Galilee. Whatever kingdom he's talking about, its not the Israel we're fighting for. Ask him why he's here. Is it because its just got too hot for him up north in Galilee with Herod Antipas?'

'You were promised this land as far back as your patriarch, Abraham, if I understand the story right. Your people have been in and around the land, but with various sets of overlords, for centuries.'

'So?' asked Barabbas.

'Well, that's the mystery to an outsider like me. On the one hand you've got the land you've been promised but for most of the time you've either been exiled or the land has been overrun or annexed. You probably count us Romans among the various foreign overlords, don't you?'

Barabbas looked at Maximus with some surprise. He hadn't met a Roman who had ever bothered to consider the history of Israel. 'So what's the mystery?' he asked.

'Where is Israel's God? That's the mystery,' replied Maximus. 'It's just not right, is it? You're in the land in some senses but still in exile in others. Not only physically, either. Israel sees itself as God's people with an expectation of a better age to come. Yet your God is silent. Where is your God?'

'We also know that through our suffering will come our vindication,' replied Barabbas. 'Some of the Maccabees died horribly but God vindicated them and the land became ours again. On the last day those martyrs too will rise to new life. If we die at your hands the same will happen for us.'

'Do you know how that will work?'

'That's probably part of the mystery,' replied Barabbas with a smile. 'Life is full of mysteries. There's a saying that if you save a life, you save all of humanity. In one sense it doesn't make sense but in another sense such individual acts make the world better. You talked about Jeshua? He teaches people to pray "God's will be done on earth as it is in heaven." How does that work? It's a mystery too. But remember: "My ways are not your ways, my thoughts are not your thoughts," says the Lord.'

'That's from your prophet Isaiah, I believe.'

'Very good, Roman,' nodded Barabbas with surprise.

'Life does indeed have its mysteries,' smiled Maximus. 'Conveniently enough you have the chance to save a life now. Maybe an innocent one.'

Barabbas looked suspiciously at him.

'You know that I am not in intelligence. I'm a front-line soldier. I captured you because that's what I do. Other people are paid to worry about what you know. But you know something which I need to know. When we captured you there were four of you. Everything being equal, the four of you will all share the same fate and that's not mine to influence. The Governor, however, has asked me about the boy who was wounded. Whatever I recommend to the Governor will probably happen to him. How did he come to be with you that morning?'

Barabbas raised an eyebrow but said nothing.

'If you say nothing I will assume that he was one of your men,' continued Maximus after a few moments of silence. 'The next time you meet him will be on the cross next to you. I will ensure that he knows you could have told me that he was innocent. Then you'll have plenty of time to explain to him why he is being crucified with you.'

Barabbas stared at him with a glimmer of calculation in his eyes. Maximus waited but Barabbas obviously decided to say nothing. Eventually Maximus spoke again.

'Is he one of your men, then?' pressed Maximus. Barabbas was silent.

'As I said,' said Maximus finally. 'I am going to take your silence as confirmation that he was one of your fighters. That means he'll be crucified with you.'

CHAPTER 20

To Maximus' eyes the Intelligence office didn't exactly inspire confidence. The first impression were the scrolls scattered across the four desks. Several shelves exhibited similar chaos. Noticing the number of plates and cups around the place he wondered who last cleaned anything. He had long suffered those doing intelligence work muttering at him about "needing to know" when he had wanted information. Today his long-suffering sense of humour wondered if they merely assumed that, if they couldn't find anything then neither could the enemy. If this office was an example of best practice in military intelligence, then it wasn't such a surprise that military plans rarely survived contact with the enemy.

A young officer glanced up as he entered the room and greeted him with a cheery: 'Morning, Centurion,' and carried on writing on the parchment in front of him. There were two other soldiers in the office and they glanced up but, following their leader's example, barely acknowledged Maximus.

'Good morning, Gaius Marcus Severus,' said Maximus, with a slightly cold tone. 'Busy?'

'The Prefect has asked for an intelligence update on the zealots at the brief tonight.' Severus kept writing as he wrote, too busy to notice Maximus' tone. 'We're just doing the summary now.' The Centurion pulled over a stool and sat himself in front of the young Roman. He leaned forward, putting his elbows on the other side of Severus' desk and waited.

Severus looked up and then Maximus saw a trace of a uncertainty enter the young man's eyes. 'Sorry, Centurion. Can I help you?'

'Better!' smiled Maximus with enough ice to keep Severus' eyes fixed to his. 'Yes, you can. Barabbas has been a guest of yours since my men brought him in, hasn't he?'

'Oh yes! He has and we've got lots of useful information from him,' nodded Severus with a smile. 'Most of which he probably doesn't realise he's given us. Intelligence is all about putting together small bits of information to make a bigger picture, as you know,' he added in a conspiratorial tone. 'That's the bigger picture we're going to be briefing Pilate about.'

'The Prefect will be thrilled no doubt,' smiled Maximus, deciding to ignore Severus' patronising tone. 'Did you know that the Prefect asked me to look into the status of one of Barabbas' men?'

'No, we didn't,' replied Severus, mystified.

'Pity. He's interested in the boy who is unconscious. Name of Benjamin, from Tiberias? Did you know that was his name?

'Possibly', said Severus, struggling, 'I think we saw his parents last week.'

'And what did you do with the information they had?'

'Well, it wasn't really that important. If they're telling the truth the boy doesn't matter.'

'So why is he still in custody?' asked Maximus.

'Why would we release him? You brought him in as a captive.'

'Do you have any reason to doubt his parents' story?

'No, Centurion, not really.'

'And did Barabbas say anything about him?'

'Not really. We've been asking him about much more important things than who happened to be with him when you caught him.'

'Did you ask the other men about him?'

'Again, not really. It's Barabbas we're interested in.'

'Are the other men really zealots, by the way?'

'Definitely. No doubt. We do know their story,' said Severus, relieved to be able to say something substantial rather than suffer more of the Centurion's questions. 'They're on the run from creditors and have been fighting with Barabbas. They've been giving us information and hoping that we won't crucify them. We don't really know much about the boy because he's been unconscious.'

'Has either of them confirmed the boy's parents' story?' asked Maximus.

'Actually the parents confirmed what little we learned from them, Centurion. They said the boy turned up just before you did.'

'So didn't it occur to you that we should release the boy to his parents?'

'As I said, that's not a decision we'd make. We just provide intelligence for others.'

'So which others would want to hear your thoughts on the matter, do you think?' asked Maximus.

'Well, you might, I suppose,' suggested Severus.

'Probably not me alone but I'm the sort of person who might recommend to the Prefect suitable courses of action in such cases, aren't I?'

'Um, yes, Centurion.'

'So should you be providing me with some intelligence then?'

'Well, er, yes, Centurion,' acknowledged Severus, increasingly uncomfortable that Maximus clearly wasn't asking these questions out of idle curiosity.

'So am I likely to be impressed when the Prefect *tells me* that a highly influential Hebrew lawyer has asked for the boy's release?' Maximus leaned a little closer into the intelligence man's face. 'And am I likely to be impressed when the Prefect *tells me* that a major member of the Sanhedrin has made the same representation? How impressed do you think *I am* when I then discover that you saw the boy's parents more than a week ago, then just left them in the corridors? How impressed do you think *I am* to hear, a week later, that we know of no reason for holding him and that you haven't bothered to tell anyone?'

'Not very impressed?' suggested Severus lamely.

Maximus stood and smashed a fist onto his desk.

'No, I'm not very impressed!' he shouted. A cup rolled off the desk onto the floor and smashed. 'Forget how you would feel if you were sitting in a dungeon for no reason with your leg hanging off! Its Passover coming, you idiots! We've only just put down the last insurrection. If we hang an innocent youth when the city is full of pilgrims a bloody riot might be the least of our problems! Especially if we hang a boy whose case has now got the backing of the high and mighty in the Sanhedrin and the Temple.'

'Sorry, Centurion,' Severus smiled weakly.

'Sorry? You're supposed to be our intelligence, aren't you?' Maximus stormed at the three of them. 'And you can't figure that one out for yourselves? And you wonder why real soldiers think military intelligence is a contradiction in terms?'

All three of them were paying attention now, Maximus noted with satisfaction. He dropped the volume to a more normal quiet tone as he continued: 'If there is good reason to keep him, I want to know within one hour. Can you do that?'

'Yes, Centurion.'

'Thank you. Back to work then, Severus,' said Maximus calmly and strode out smiling to himself. He refrained from ill-tempered rants since he found such violence generally unproductive. He kept an eye out for the odd occasions when he was justified in shouting at someone though, ideally every year or so. He knew the word would get around and remind everyone that he could.

'Oh, just one more thing,' asked Maximus quietly as he turned back from the door. 'Did you know the boy is conscious again?

'No, Centurion. That would mean that we could talk to him.'

'I'm sure you could do it in time to get whatever you learn in your recommendations to me within an hour, couldn't you?'

'Leave it to me, Centurion.' Severus assured him. 'And I'm sorry we didn't think about telling you that we'd seen the boy's parents.'

'Thank you,' acknowledged Maximus, turning to leave. Then he turned back again.

'When you've spoken to the boy, then will you go and ask Barabbas to confirm the story. Then come and tell me *exactly* what Barabbas tells you.'

There must be a reason why Barabbas refused to confirm what everyone else apparently agrees on, thought Maximus. He quietly closed the door behind him. As he walked back to his office he made a mental note to suggest that the Prefect might like to make a surprise visit to Severus and his team.

CHAPTER 21

Just under an hour later Severus arrived with his report.

'We spoke to the boy and they sound like they've all got the same story. He was kidnapped, he escaped, he stumbled across Barabbas' and the other two, then you turned up and arrested them all.'

'Take a seat, Severus.' Maximus indicated a couple of stools and Severus brought one across the room and sat down in front of Maximus' desk. 'So can I tell the Prefect we have no reason to hold the boy?'

'I can't see a reason from the evidence we have,' replied Severus. 'We have no reason to doubt any of them, except for what Barabbas himself said'.

'What did he say?'

'He's refused to confirm the boy's story.'

'You mean he has said something different, or he's just keeping quiet. That's why I asked you to tell me exactly what he said.'

'I know you did. So we wrote it down exactly as you asked.' Severus produced a small scroll.

'We started by asking him who his three friends were. To which he replied that the men taken with him are fellow soldiers fighting against pagans.'

'Were those his actual words?'

'His actual words.'

'Did you ask about the boy specifically?'

'Yes I did. I asked him how the boy came to be with him in the camp. He just repeated that the men taken with him are soldiers fighting against pagans.'

'The same words again?'

'Yes,' nodded Severus. 'I then told him that there was a story that the boy only joined the camp just before they were all arrested. That the boy was nothing to do with the uprising and would he, Barabbas, like to comment?'

'What was his answer?' asked Maximus. 'No, don't tell me. "The men captured with me are all soldiers fighting against pagans."'

'That's right, Centurion. Exactly that,' confirmed Severus.

'Did he say anything else?

'No,' Severus shook his head. 'All I got was the same phrase.'

'What does that tell us?' asked Maximus.

'Either the boy and everyone else is lying but they've got some powerful people to believe them. Or Barabbas isn't actually telling a lie but he's not telling us the whole truth. He won't confirm the boy's innocence, for some reason, but nor will he say he's a brigand.'

'But why?' asked Maximus.

'Barabbas thinks there's some benefit to us crucifying an innocent?' Severus speculated.

'That's the best I can think of,' Maximus agreed. 'If we give them an innocent martyr, as well as Barabbas and his fellow brigands, and at Passover too, then the zealots might think they can call for a much bigger uprising than they could otherwise manage. Are you aware of the significance of the death of innocents at Passover?'

'No, not really,' said Severus, leaning forward with interest.

'Passover celebrates the Hebrews being freed from

slavery in Egypt centuries ago. The legend is that their leader, a man called Moses, sent them home to prepare to travel, telling each family to quickly make some unleavened bread and to kill a lamb to eat. The blood of the lamb was then daubed on the doors of each Hebrew house as a mark that they were God's people. That night their God sent a destroyer through Egypt to kill every firstborn. Wherever the blood of the innocent lamb was painted on the door of the house, the destroyer passed over, hence the name of the festival they're about to celebrate.'

'So Barabbas could be using young Benjamin as an innocent sacrifice to rouse the Hebrew people to rise against us, you mean?'

'Maybe,' nodded Maximus. 'It's not a particularly exact parallel with their Exodus story but he might think it's the best he can do from inside our dungeon.'

Severus grimaced in disgust. 'What a nasty piece of work.'

CHAPTER 22

Jerusalem: Pilate's office in the Herodian Palace, Monday evening

'Centurion?' Pilate greeted Maximus, acknowledging a salute.

'The boy from Tiberias, Prefect. You wanted me to investigate the circumstances which led to him being in Barabbas' camp when we arrested them.'

'Oh, yes. The boy Nicodemus told me was innocent.'

'I spoke to Barabbas, the men with him, the boy and his parents. Severus also spoke to Barabbas. I gather he briefed you on intelligence matters this afternoon?

'Does the picture we've got match the stories that Nicodemus and the lawyer Eleazar told me?' asked Pilate.

'It does, Prefect,' replied Maximus. 'Barabbas won't say the boy turned up just before we did but he refuses to deny it. I think that's because he hopes that an innocent dying, especially at Passover, could be a powerful symbol for the zealots to rally behind in establishing their independent kingdom.'

'What! You think he's happy to sacrifice the boy for his own political ends?'

'It looks that way,' confirmed Maximus.

'I suppose that's the sort of people we're up against here.' Pilate shook his head with disgust. 'If this afternoon's intelligence picture is accurate, it might have been Barabbas' group that kidnapped the boy in the first place.'

'Do you want me to release the boy then?' asked Maximus.

Pilate thought for a moment. Maximus looked at the Prefect and waited.

'No. We will try him with Barabbas and the others and Roman justice will prevail if there is no real evidence against him. You have his parents?'

'Yes, Prefect. They're staying near the city.'

'Then Eleazar will no doubt speak in his defence and they will be witnesses. Do we have a trial date for Barabbas and his men?'

'Thursday I think, Sir.'

'Thursday it is, Centurion. Well done again and thank you.'

Maximus smiled, saluted and left to return to the Antonia Fortress.

PART FOUR

WEDNESDAY BEFORE PASSOVER

CHAPTER 23

Jerusalem, Wednesday morning

Wednesday morning again found Maximus walking briskly behind his troops along the trading arcade that ran under the western wall of the Jerusalem Temple Mount. A zealot was reported to be attacking the Temple stall-holders who sold animals for sacrifices and exchanged legal tender for the "sacred" coinage that the Temple insisted be used to buy them.

Pilgrims always grumbled about the margins charged by the cartels of licensed traders. Maximus had observed that such religious cartels usually found reasons for charging premium prices too and dismissing any complaints as putting money before righteousness.

His soldiers pushed people out of the way but as the pavement narrowed progress slowed and then halted. Maximus saw two loose animals thrashing about in panic. They had escaped from trading booths just inside the Temple entrances and headed straight onto the pavements outside. A young couple were helping an injured man who hobbled past them with a bleeding head-wound. Lucius though, was seeing the funny side: Maximus heard the words "orgy" and "brothel" in a negative-sounding comment about the Temple's organisational skills.

'At least the cattle can't stampede in this crush,' joked one soldier to another, leaning on their spears at the back of the column. There was nothing for them to do and no immediate possibility of injury.

'A sheep could give you a nasty nip, though,' replied the soldier by his side. 'Think what height the average sheep keeps his head at.' There was a ripple of laughter amongst the troops and some invective comments from the crowd. Being Samaritans they were hated by the locals almost more than the Romans. The soldiers just sneered: they reckoned no one would dare actually to throw a punch. Maximus smiled at the image of being savaged at genital height by a frightened sheep, but pointed out to the men that this was not a good place to risk a fight. Apart from a joke about losing bullocks, the soldiers stopped talking and smirked at each other instead.

'Somebody must have been really upset,' Lucius mused as they waited.

'So it seems,' said Maximus. 'Funny isn't it? If these religious traders believed in a god, wouldn't they try to supply their fellow worshippers with things at something around the best price?'

'Religious suppliers have got to eat too, though,' Lucius pointed out.

'Yes, but there's a difference between making a decent living and extortion, isn't there? Does it really cost *that* much more to grow animals for sacrifice? Do they eat more grass or something?'

'I don't know,' Lucius shrugged. He wasn't a farmer either.

Eventually the crowd was pushed back and Maximus and Lucius followed the troops up the steps and into the southern end of the Temple courts. Temple guards were helping the traders to round up stray animals. The pilgrims still waiting to purchase sacrifices had been dispersed away from the booths in the south-western corner of the Temple Mount. Across the clear area, Maximus saw Jonathan who was studying the traders rebuilding their stands.

CHAPTER 24

Jerusalem, the Temple courts, Wednesday morning

'Looks like we missed the excitement,' said Maximus as the two Romans joined Jonathan. 'What happened?'

'Jeshua of Nazareth happened,' replied Jonathan glumly. 'He attacked the money changers and the animal sellers. Apparently he started whipping them with a rope and throwing things about. Some animals escaped. He knocked over some birdcages which burst open. Obviously we won't get those birds back.'

'Why would Jeshua attack the Temple?' asked Lucius. 'Isn't he a devout rabbi?'

'Apparently he thinks we're turning the Temple into a den of thieves. I gather some in the crowd agreed with him too.' Jonathan saw Lucius and Maximus exchange knowing looks. 'Do you know something I don't?' enquired Jonathan;

'No, not particularly' answered Maximus, looking around at the scene. 'As we were coming over we were wondering if the prices these traders charge were excessive, that's all. If so, is it any wonder he's popular?' The Romans smiled at each other and Jonathan laughed.

'I can't comment on prices, Maximus. You know the pressures involved.'

'You mean I know because I'm a long-suffering victim of the righteous? I surely do,' Maximus laughed slightly cynically. 'So you've arrested Jeshua then?'

'Er, no,' replied Jonathan hesitatingly. Maximus noticed a troubled look. 'He's a popular figure,' Jonathan went on slightly dismissively. 'Its nearly Passover, and this was an isolated incident. It's safer to ignore it for now. No harm done.'

'So long as you weren't the chap with the broken head,' observed Lucius.

'Many more would have been hurt if we'd arrested him and had a riot in that confined area.' Jonathan pointed out.

'I see what you mean,' Lucius nodded, glancing along the pavement. The pilgrims were flooding back and the traders were anxious to get back to business.

'So has Jeshua left?' asked Maximus.

'No, he's still in the Temple.'

'You've let him stay in the Temple?' Maximus looked at him in amazement. 'Are you sure he won't cause more trouble?'

'Oh, that's unlikely,' replied Jonathan. 'It was the way the traders were carrying on that upset him. He won't attack the Temple itself. Would you excuse me, Centurion? I do need to report to the High Priest.'

'Of course,' nodded Maximus, 'if there's nothing more we can do then we'll get away too. Let us know if we can help.'

'We will,' said Jonathan. He smiled at the two Roman officers and called two of his own officers. The three of them walked briskly away.

Maximus and Lucius looked at each other, then returned to the pavement outside the Temple where the decanus was waiting.

'Don't think there's anything for us to do, Sir. It was that man Jeshua of Nazareth. Cross at the prices being charged or something. He's still in the Temple and no one there wants to do anything either. Unless you have any other instructions, Sir, may I get the men back to barracks?'

'Yes. Carry on.' The decanus saluted and walked away, calling his men. Aware of Maximus' watchful eye, they responded smartly. A minute or so later the Roman detachment marched off towards the Antonia Fortress the way they had come.

As the officers followed the troops back along the pavement beside the western wall of the Temple Mount, Maximus observed discreetly to Lucius: 'I think the High Priest is worried that Jeshua is becoming too popular.'

'Shouldn't we have arrested him?' asked Lucius.

'If he'd been outside the Temple courts, maybe. Best not to charge inside without an invitation from the High Priest. We're trying to avoid trouble. I think doing nothing about a few money-changers' tables tossed over is consistent with that aim.'

'True,' Lucius agreed. 'Who'd run to help a money-changer?'

'You know,' Maximus went on, 'I would love to be at the meeting Jonathan's about to have with the High Priest. That's twice in two weeks I've seen him looking very shifty. Both times it's been about Jeshua of Nazareth.'

CHAPTER 25

Jerusalem, the High Priest's office, the Temple,
Wednesday morning

Jonathan was standing too much at attention for his own liking as he explained to Annas his handling of Jeshua's sudden attack on the Temple traders.

'By the time I arrived it was all over,' he said. 'The traders were arguing with him about his authority but the crowd was mainly on his side. My first instinct was to arrest him but there could have been serious trouble. The Romans were on their way so any more violence would have drawn them in too.'

Jonathan could see that Annas was unhappy. Jeshua had already escaped once before, so it was annoying that Jonathan couldn't arrest him now that he was openly in the city. Looking from the window into the courts, Annas saw crowds milling about where he imagined Jeshua was teaching at that moment. He had no doubt that a man so idolised by the mob did threaten the Temple.

'Did Jeshua actually have anyone with him when he arrived in the trading area?' Annas asked.

'Some disciples, the group they call the Twelve, I expect.'

'Did anyone notice whether he brought this whip with

him? That suggests pre-meditation? Or did he just pick up some rope that was there? That suggests he's a hot-head with a violent streak.'

'I don't know,' Jonathan admitted. The question hadn't occurred to him.

'Were all the animals re-captured?'

'The sheep and cattle, yes,' Jonathan replied, 'Not the birds, obviously. Apart from that, there was no long term loss or damage.' Jonathan paused then added: 'That was another reason why I didn't risk inflaming the situation.'

Annas turned back to the window and resumed watching the crowds below: 'We'd better compensate those who lost livestock. Fortunately birds are quite cheap but I wouldn't want to pay for a herd of sacrificial quality cattle. Meanwhile Jeshua has hundreds of pilgrims lapping up his every word, by the look of it.'

The doors swung open and Joseph marched in looking less than serene. He ordered the slaves outside and to close the doors. This conference was not to be disturbed. When the three of them were alone he turned to Jonathan,

'Jeshua is on the Temple Mount again and I am told he just attacked some money changers and some animal sellers.'

'Yes, Sir,' replied Jonathan, mentally steeling himself to justify again why he hadn't arrested Jeshua there and then.

Joseph, though, had already worked out why. 'I assume it was too dangerous to try to arrest him?' he asked, but without waiting for an answer he joined Annas at the window and they both peered down at the crowds below them. Joseph looked back at Jonathan and pointed at a large section of the crowd: 'Hence this little festival of his own?' There was a sarcastic tone in his question. Jonathan was uncertain what to say but again Joseph didn't wait for an answer.

'He has too many supporters with him for now,' he went on. The walk from the Temple itself had given him time to consider a plan. 'If we can't arrest him then we must undermine his message.' He thought for a few moments. 'Did you hear what he said to the traders?' he asked.

'Something about turning the Temple into a den of thieves, I was told,' Jonathan offered.

'Nothing so bland, I'm afraid,' laughed Joseph,

'Really, so what did he say?' asked Annas.

'Jeshua is very clever,' replied Joseph. 'One of the scribes made some notes for me. He said "It is written that my house will be a house of prayer but you have made it a den of brigands."

'Does he think the Temple is just where we hide from God like thieves?' asked Jonathan, aghast.

'Jeshua didn't say "thieves". He said "brigands": robbers for political gain. Jeshua's alluding to two pieces of scripture. In the prophecy of Isaiah the Lord says the Temple should "be a house of worship for all nations" but Jeshua accused us instead of turning the Temple into exactly "the den of robbers" that the prophet Jeremiah objected to in his day. Instead of bringing the nations to God, he's saying we're just like the zealots who rob to finance violence against the gentiles, in this case the Romans.'

'What does he expect us to do?' asked Annas angrily. 'This land is Hebrew land. Its ours from God. How else are we ever going to get it cleansed of pagans?'

'Be that as it may,' said Joseph, not wishing to be diverted to a discussion of Temple support for rebellion against the Romans, 'Jeshua has given me an idea about how we're to deal with him.'

'Ah!' said Annas, 'What have you in mind?'

'He's attacking us now on theological grounds. He's

quoting scripture at us. We have the finest brains in Judah here, don't we?' Joseph asked.

'Oh, good idea,' replied Annas, the gleam in his eye suggesting that he had latched onto Joseph' chain of thought. 'He may impress the good folk of Galilee but we can tie him up over theology. How about resurrection, for instance?' Annas smiled at the thought of engaging with Jeshua's views on resurrection. It was a popular subject of dispute between various Hebrew factions. 'When he says something stupid, his support will vanish as fast as it appeared, especially if we can put people in the crowd to amplify his errors.'

'Exactly,' nodded Joseph, 'and we can make sure that news spreads quickly through the city.' Joseph turned back to Jonathan 'How did the crowd react to the attacks?' he asked.

'Most of them cheered him on,' replied Jonathan.

'Inevitable, I fear,' nodded Joseph philosophically,

'There's no respect for proper religion today,' scowled Annas, 'especially among young people. That's probably why he's surrounded by youths.'

'What Jeshua forgets, Jonathan,' said Joseph, 'is that there are many who see payment for the sacrament as part of expressing their faith. Otherwise it's not a sacrifice. Some priests talk about making the faith more accessible, but there are still lots of people who value ritual because it is prescribed in Torah.' Joseph looked back at the crowds broodingly. 'Is Eleazar in Jerusalem at the moment?' asked Joseph.

'He told me he'll be available at short notice,' Jonathan confirmed.

'Good,' Joseph smiled. 'Speed suits us. The Festival is only two days away and we need to disorientate Jeshua. He's clever but a tradesman from Galilee won't be *that* clever.'

Joseph turned to Jonathan: 'Time for Eleazar's adversarial skills. Could you find him and get him here as soon as possible,' Jonathan acknowledged them both and left the room to send for the lawyer. Then Joseph looked back to Annas, 'Food, I think!'

CHAPTER 26

Jerusalem, the High Priest's office, the Temple,
Wednesday afternoon

Eleazar had been scandalised by news of Jeshua's conduct in the centre of the Hebrew faith. Annas and Joseph took chairs at the heads of the low table and at Joseph' invitation Eleazar settled on one of the couches that was drawn along one side. He looked relaxed but alert. Reuben, his assistant, occupied a couch opposite and was ready to take notes. Jonathan sat next to him. At a signal from Annas, the slaves left the room. Jonathan opened the meeting by summarising that morning's attack on the traders' booths.

'It's appalling that this Galilean comes here, supposedly teaching about the God of Abraham and Moses and then attacks the Temple itself. What sort of Hebrew does he think he is?' Eleazar sipped on a drink and looked at Joseph. 'Have you any thoughts about a preferred approach?'

'Nothing must interfere with the Passover ceremonies,' replied Joseph, 'We need Jeshua neutralised so that he can't disrupt things. It's as simple as that.'

'That's very succinct,' Eleazar acknowledged. 'Can I clarify something? I see why, given the number of lambs that need to be slaughtered within the time available, efficiency is essential. Disrupting the trade causes chaos but I doubt your real concern here is that pilgrims are kept waiting too long to make their sacrifices, is it? He's effectively accusing the Temple of using the sacrificial system for profit?'

'The most important threat comes from the question of authority,' said the High Priest. 'The way Jeshua conducts his ministry here undermines the good order of the faith. His claims to be anointed are clear, to Jews anyway. Thankfully the Romans are oblivious so far. He is producing supposed miracles that challenge the natural order of things. He even includes women in his retinue for instance. He accords them a status and appoints them to roles that God never envisaged for women. In doing so he undermines the natural authority of men. It's as we discussed at dinner the other night.'

'Are his wonders fake or real?' wondered Eleazar.

'How can anyone tell?' asked Annas. 'Jeshua might be a trickster or an illusionist. There nothing to stop him planning large-scale illusions, is there?'

'Which would make him a simple charlatan.' observed Eleazar.

'Precisely. Of course Jeshua might be a sorcerer. Don't forget Moses was confronted with Pharaoh's sorcerers who did wonders too. Whatever power or trickery he employs, his teaching is undermining the authority of the Temple. He is challenging the interpretations of righteousness that we have been teaching since Moses. If he really was anointed he wouldn't be doing that, would he?' There were nods of agreement.

'Misleading the people is punishable by death under Mosaic Law,' said Eleazar. 'I've also been told he has women still married to other men among his followers. Is that right?' The two priests looked at each other and smiled.

'Including Pilate's wife, as it happens,' said Annas and Eleazar's eyebrows raised, 'not that Claudia Procula would allow herself to be compromised. But yes. And many of his followers sleep together on the road. Most rabbis teach that women can endanger men. Hence the need for them to be controlled by fathers or husbands. Jeshua's behaviour is unseemly.'

Joseph then leaned forward and looked at Eleazar: 'Imagine if a daughter of yours was one of them.' Eleazar wrinkled his nose in distaste at the thought and Joseph continued: 'Even if she returned to the family, how would you ever be able to marry her well? Imagine the chaos in society if we all abandoned proper manners like that.'

'I see what you mean,' Eleazar said, echoing the disgust in Joseph' voice. 'We've considered taking him for adultery, I assume? It is also a capital crime under Mosaic law.'

'There are no witnesses or aggrieved husbands that we know of. Don't forget that the equality he offers women he also offers to all sorts of unrighteous people: tax collectors and collaborators with the Romans, prostitutes, various lepers…'

'An example might help,' interposed Annas, 'if I may, Joseph?' Joseph deferred to Annas. 'One woman with him here, I gather, joined his band in Galilee. God cursed her with a permanent bleed for years. She was literally untouchable by any righteous Hebrew. The story is she touched him[25].'

'Why would a rabbi allow himself to be made unclean?' asked Eleazar, mystified.

'Exactly,' agreed Annas, 'but he did and this woman was apparently healed of the bleed.'

'I hear that if he does heal someone who is sick, he sends them to the priests in the normal way,' said Eleazar.

'Well that's hardly an endorsement of the Temple's

authority, is it?' Joseph snorted, leaning back and adjusting his clothes in frustration. 'The key theological point though: Jeshua claims to forgive their sins.'

'I'm surprised no one has stoned him,' said Eleazar.

'People have tried,' said Joseph, 'but he's always escaped. Lots of his people feel because they are now healed they are righteous again. So many that follow him are healed sinners that they think, by extension, that Jeshua has the Lord's authority to forgive sin.'

'If you've been bleeding all your life you don't have much to leave behind if you go with him, do you?' mused Eleazar. 'Where was her husband? But then who would have married her? How did she live?'

'Prostitution probably,' replied Annas.

'I suspect the crowds *won't* stone him,' said Joseph. 'Don't forget he's telling those he has forgiven that the Lord considers them as righteous as you or I. They may be more likely to stone anyone who challenges him.'

Eleazar inhaled deeply. 'So he's become untouchable then.'

'That's why we need you to engage him in argument and expose the errors in his message,' said Annas. 'If he's publicly discredited his authority will crumble.'

Eleazar leaned forward. 'So, he is leading people away from godliness and may also be a sorcerer. I imagine the women around him are leading him astray, so to speak.' He paused in case there was anything else Joseph or Annas wanted to add. They said nothing.

'So,' he said, after a few moments reflection, 'we demonstrate publicly his lack of authority and spread the word. I have people who will help there too.'

'Where do you see he has weaknesses?' asked Annas.

'If he's proclaiming himself *messiah*, that could be sedition. The Romans take a dim view of kings. If we get him publicly to oppose Caesar, are you worried about the Romans executing him?'

Annas and Joseph looked at each other then Joseph answered: 'The loss of any Hebrew to pagans is sad but, as I said before, it is better that one man dies, than the whole nation.'

CHAPTER 27

Jerusalem: The Temple courts, Wednesday afternoon

Neither Annas, Eleazar, nor Reuben were used to pushing their way through crowds or, for that matter, being jostled back. Their rank and status meant they could normally avoid crowds but few in this crowd knew who they were. Two Temple guards were ahead of them pushing to get them to the front. They could hear Jeshua making a speech. The people were packed tightly together, shoulder to shoulder and, straining as they were to hear Jeshua, almost oblivious to anything behind them. There were some complaints too, mainly from pilgrims from abroad who did not immediately recognise either the former High Priest or the lawyers.

Eventually though, the guards got them to the front. Annas decided to stand behind Eleazar, looking over his left shoulder and the guards stood behind Annas to protect him. Eleazar straightened his clothes and saw that Jeshua had stopped speaking. Between them were several disciples seated on the ground who had turned to look at Eleazar. They seemed less than pleased at the interruption. Jeshua was leaning against a wall, arms folded over his chest, watching Eleazar and waiting for them all to stop moving.

A bad start, Eleazar decided. He glanced at the faces

watching him and smiled grimly. The crowd was facing Jeshua and he controlled their attention.

'Well, friends!' Jeshua started and Eleazar hurriedly focussed on Jeshua himself, who had pushed himself away from the wall, unfolded his arms and addressed the crowd with the air of one ignoring impoliteness. 'We are honoured today. A chief priest and his scribes have joined us.' This is getting worse, thought Eleazar, as the crowd murmured in response and the tension increased at the prospect of a clash between Jeshua and the authorities. Eleazar thought he heard a hiss from somewhere behind him as Jeshua asked: 'Can we help you, gentlemen? Is there something we can tell you?' A ripple of amusement spread though the packed crowd and Jeshua smiled gently.

'Does he really know who we are or was that just a guess?' Eleazar whispered to Reuben and Annas beside him. 'Is he just lucky or very good?' Annas stirred uncomfortably.

'Rabbi,' Eleazar called out in a clear voice measured to be heard widely. 'About your actions and your teaching this morning. Tell us by what authority you are doing these things[26]. And who gave you that authority?' The crowd buzzed again and Eleazar was delighted by applause from some parts of the crowd. Jeshua was attracting the undecided but not everyone was convinced yet. Attention switched to Jeshua who looked at Eleazar.

'I will also ask you a question,' announced Jeshua to scattered applause. 'John's baptism. Was it from heaven?' Jeshua paused then lowered his voice, 'Or from men?' Many in the crowd knew John the Baptist had often been less than complimentary about the rich and powerful. As Jeshua's question sank in there was more applause, a bit of laughter and from the back of the crowd there was a shout which, though the detail didn't quite carry to the front, Eleazar knew from the tone was directed at him and was not complimentary.

Annas' spoke close to his left ear. 'If we reply "from heaven," then Jeshua will ask why we didn't believe John. If we say "from man" we're at risk of being stoned. I suspect most of these people think that John was a prophet from God.'

'Yes, I know. It's a trap,' Eleazar whispered back to Annas. He fixed a dismissive smile on his face and cleared his throat: 'We don't know where it was from.'

There was wild applause and the crowd jeered loudly at the admission. Amid mocking laughter, Eleazar grimly looked Jeshua in the eye. Jeshua raised his hands for quiet and waited for the noise to drop. Eleazar now knew he would lose this opening exchange.

'Then I won't tell you by what authority I am doing these things,' Jeshua replied. More applause followed and more abusive remarks were aimed at Annas and the lawyers. Embarrassed but trapped at the front of the crowd they could only stand with dignity and fume with anger. Jeshua held his hands up again for quiet and attention swung back to listen to him.

CHAPTER 28

'What do you think?' Jeshua asked, pointing at the lawyers with one hand while his other swept around the crowd. Then he smiled and his tone changed as he started to tell a story[27]. 'There was a man with two sons!' As Jeshua paused Eleazar thought to himself: He's smiling because he knows he's let us off the hook for now. The crowd settled in anticipation. Jeshua was renowned for penetrating parables.

'The man said to his first son: "Go and work today in the vineyard." "I will not!" the son answered but later that day he changed his mind and went to work.' Jeshua paused and his eyes swept around the crowd. 'Meanwhile the father went to the other son and said: "Go and work today in the vineyard." 'The other son said "I will." The crowd saw Jeshua's eyes come to rest on the lawyers. 'But that son did not go.' Despite Jeshua's friendly tone, Eleazar knew they would soon be on the wrong end of this. Every Jew knew the vineyard was an often-used image for Israel.

'So,' Jeshua asked Eleazar, 'which of these two did what his father wanted?'

Eleazar's heart sank as a ripple of conversation ran around the crowd. He looked at Annas and then grimaced an aside to Reuben. 'Never ask a question you don't know the answer to. When this is over we ought to try to hire him.'

Having quoted the old trial lawyers' rule he turned back

130

to Jeshua. He could see where this was going. 'The first one of course,' Eleazar replied as the crowd became quiet, his face still locked determinedly into a smile. Jeshua smiled back.

'The first one!' Jeshua announced his acknowledgment of that answer with another sweep of his hands. 'Exactly right, Brother. The first one.' His tone was kindly. He looked so gentle and magnanimous that, if Eleazar hadn't long ago learned how to fake sincerity, he would have believed Jeshua was being friendly. Suddenly Jeshua pointed at Annas and the lawyers.

'And I tell you the truth. The tax collectors and the prostitutes are entering the Kingdom of God ahead of you, because John came to show you the way of righteousness and you did not believe him.' Jeshua swept his arms expansively across the crowd. 'But tax collectors and prostitutes did.' At that the crowd started to murmur, 'and even after you saw that,' Jeshua jabbed his finger back at the lawyers, 'you still didn't believe him and repent.'

There was more applause but also sounds of angry surprise. Many were shocked that anyone might suggest that God would admit prostitutes to the Kingdom before priests. They were also angry that Jeshua said it to a former High Priest.

Jeshua held up one hand for quiet, pointing at Eleazar and his companions with the other. As the crowd settled Jeshua went on:

'Listen to another parable. There was a landowner who planted a vineyard.[28]' The crowd buzzed as some recognised the story. Others though, were muttering that another vineyard story indicated another assault on the Temple. Wasn't *messiah* supposed to attack the Romans? Eleazar was also shocked at the suggestion that prostitutes might be more favoured than priests. As a trial lawyer though, he

131

marvelled at how Jeshua moved the crowd.

Jeshua's tone started light. 'The landowner built a wall around the vineyard, then a wine press and a watchtower. Then he rented the vineyard to some farmers and left for a journey. When the harvest time approached,' Jeshua lowered his voice, 'he sent his slaves to the tenants to collect his fruit.' He paused.

'The tenants seized his slaves. They beat one. They killed another. They stoned a third. So the owner sent other slaves to them, more this time and the tenants treated them all in the same way. So finally, he sent his own son to them. "They will respect my son" the landowner told himself.'

Jeshua paused and looked around the crowd, picking out and catching the eyes of different individuals before he continued. 'But when the tenants saw the son they said to each other: "This is the heir. Let's kill him and take his inheritance". So they threw him out of the vineyard and killed him.' The crowd were still. 'When the owner of the vineyard comes back,' asked Jeshua, with a pause as he looked around the crowd, 'what will he do to those tenants?' Then Jeshua looked Eleazar in the eye once more.

'He will bring them to a wretched end!' a voice cried out in the crowd. 'He'll rent the vineyard to tenants who will give him his share.' called another.

'Exactly!' Jeshua said. 'Have you never read in the scriptures, "The stone the builders have rejected has become the capstone, the Lord has done this and it is marvellous in our eyes?" I'm telling you, the vineyard will be taken away from you and given to a people who will produce his fruit. He who falls on this stone will be broken to pieces but he on whom it falls will be crushed.' There was applause but mixed with some abusive comment.

Annas, on impulse,[29] asked a question of his own: 'Rabbi, Moses wrote that if a man's brother dies and leaves a wife without child then his brother should take the wife and raise offspring for his brother. There were seven brothers: the first took a wife and died without raising a child, so the second took her. But he died without leaving seed also.'

There was murmuring as many had recognised Annas. Here was a Sadducee asking Jeshua about resurrection; they sensed a good argument to come. Most of them knew that the Sadducees didn't believe in any life after death, unlike most of the many Pharisees in the crowd. They looked forward to hearing Jeshua's view. Annas continued:

'All seven eventually took her but died without leaving offspring. Then, the woman herself died. In the resurrection whose wife will she be?' There was applause at the question and Annas smiled around him in acknowledgment. He glanced at Eleazar, who acknowledged the skill of the question. The crowd hushed. Would Jeshua defend resurrection when Annas had just made it sound absurd? Jeshua, instead, undermined the basis of the question:

'Why are you wrong?' said Jeshua with a shake of his head. 'You don't know the scriptures nor the power of God.' A buzz went around the crowd as those who recognised Annas explained to others that a Galilean had just said that to a former High Priest. Jeshua held up his hand. When the crowd quietened enough he continued:

'It is true that the children of *this* age do marry. They are given in marriage. But those who are worthy to take part in the age to come and in the resurrection of the dead cannot die any more. They won't marry or be given in marriage.'

The crowd murmured at this. That was new. Does it mean that marriage is only for this life, they wondered? Jeshua seemed to know the questions they were asking. The immortality of the righteous in the age to come would make things different.

'The dead are raised,' Jeshua assured them, looking at Annas. 'Did you never read in the book of Moses, in the passage about the bush? He speaks of the Lord as the God of Abraham, the God of Isaac and the God of Jacob? God is not God of the dead, but of the living.' Jeshua shook his head again, 'No, you are quite wrong.'

The crowd applauded thoughtfully. A buzz of conversation suggested they were still digesting this train of thought. Eleazar was lost in thought too: so the present age will be replaced by an "age to come" in which the righteous will rise to new life. The Pharisees already agreed with Jeshua about that. The marriage angle was new though. Eleazar had heard Annas' argument many times before but it had always seemed just a rather obvious reduction to the ridiculous. Jeshua had made a practical sense of it though. Marriage was about the orderly passage of property through the generations in this world. So if people in God's Kingdom in the next age didn't die, will people married in this world no longer be married to each other in the age to come? Suddenly Eleazar's thoughts were interrupted by a sharp tug on his robe. Annas whispered angrily:

'There's nothing more we can do here and I'm not staying to be insulted any more. We're going.' Eleazar caught Reuben's eye, indicating that they should follow Annas. As the crowd saw them push their way back through the people there was a burst of ribald applause. Eleazar glanced back at Jeshua. He was still and silent as he watched them leave.

CHAPTER 29

Jerusalem, the High Priest's office, the Temple,
Wednesday afternoon

Annas was seething as they returned to the High Priest's rooms. He snatched the cup of water offered by the slave who greeted them. Scowling, he crossed to the window without a word and looked out into the Temple courts beneath him. Eleazar exchanged some quiet words with Reuben, who nodded and left the room. He joined Annas by the window.

'We came off second best there,' admitted Eleazar a little glumly.

'That's rather an understatement,' said Annas, crisply. 'Who does that man think he is? He's publicly insulting the priesthood. How can we protect the people from the pagans if that man undermines everything that we do? He's telling people that the Temple is as much of a problem to God as the Romans are and everyone in that crowd knows that is what he means. Next thing he'll have the mob marching against us.'

'I'm sure you're right,' agreed Eleazar, who knew Annas understood that legal actions, like wars, are rarely won during the first engagement. 'But we've learned plenty about him and given nothing away. I think I can see our next step.' He knew how to calm down clients after a bad day in court. Annas looked at him enquiringly.

'What have you in mind?' he asked.

'Well, we've confirmed that he sees himself as a prophet,' Eleazar smiled. He had used the walk back to good effect. 'You said it yourself, he does indeed see the Temple is as much of a problem to God as the pagans. We know his vineyard parable is one of his most popular stories about the failure of Israel to honour God. The prophets said much the same to Israel before the exile. "Let those with ears hear". He's claiming to be the son in that parable he just told about us. For those with ears he is saying that he is bringing God's Kingdom into being himself. He's claiming to be the son returning to reclaim the vineyard for God his father.'

'Yes,' snapped Annas, unable to keep exasperation out of his voice. 'I know he tells that parable quite often and I know what it means too. So what?'

'He's now given us the statement that we can use to trap him. How is Jeshua's Kingdom going to relate to Caesar's Kingdom? The Romans will be very interested in Jeshua's answer to that question. So I suggest we ask it in public. The Romans will deal with him if he says something that challenges Caesar's rule. By claiming to be the son of the vineyard owner he's telling us that is precisely what he intends.'

'Jeshua is Lord, Caesar is not!' Annas almost savoured the phrase. 'You've a plan then?'

'Oh yes!' Eleazar smiled positively. 'We ask him in public whether he thinks we should pay taxes to Caesar. The crowd know that when Judah the Galilean revolted he refused to pay taxes to Caesar. Their grandfathers will have told them about Judah Maccabee. The crowd won't accept him as anointed if he sides *with* pagans by supporting Roman taxes. But if Jeshua says "no" to paying taxes, then he commits sedition. Then the Romans execute him as another rebel. Either way, problem solved.'

Annas took the point. 'When do you propose to engage him again then?'

'Now. Then either way it will be around the city by nightfall. I've just sent for a few colleagues to be credible witnesses.'

'Many of Jeshua's actions have taken place in Galilee. What if he asks to be tried by Herod as Tetrarch of Galilee?' asked Annas. 'The Tetrarch is a Hebrew too, don't forget.' Eleazar had already seen the jurisdiction issue.

'I've also sent for a colleague who is one of Herod's courtiers. I doubt Herod would be any easier on Jeshua but if Herod is scared that Jeshua might be John the Baptist back from the dead, he won't be keen to execute him again will he?' Eleazar and Annas both laughed at the thought. 'It shouldn't be difficult to persuade Herod to leave Jeshua to us and the Romans.'

'Does Herod actually care about Jeshua, do you think?'

'Herod wants to be acknowledged as anointed himself. He also has the same economic and political interest in maintaining the *status quo* that you Sadducees do. Whatever kingdom Jeshua wants to build, Herod won't be king of it, will he?'

'No. I imagine not,' agreed Annas.

CHAPTER 30

Jerusalem: the Temple courts, Wednesday afternoon

Later that afternoon Eleazar returned to the crowds. Annas chose to forego another encounter with Jeshua; Eleazar and Reuben were instead accompanied by three prominent Pharisees and two of Herod's courtiers.

The crowds were thinner that late in the afternoon. Eleazar waited until Jeshua was moving towards the exits and positioned himself so that Jeshua came towards the lawyers. A large crowd were still with him, some chatting with Jeshua.

Jeshua, however, had seen Eleazar ahead of him and, having answered a question from someone on his left, he raised a hand and greeted Eleazar:

'Teacher of Israel! We meet again. You are well?'

Eleazar replied with a smile: 'Indeed I am, Rabbi. If I may, we have another question for you. A conundrum upon which many of us would like your advice[30].' A compliment, Eleazar judged, cost them nothing. Jeshua had stopped about six feet in front of him. His disciples and the rest of the crowd closed around them, those at the back straining to hear.

'Teacher, we know you are a man of integrity,' Eleazar began in a loud voice that the crowd could all hear. 'We know you are not swayed by men, because you pay no attention to who they are. You teach the way of God in accordance with the truth.' Eleazar could see Jeshua knew the opening was sheer affectation. 'Is it right we should pay taxes to Caesar or not?' asked Eleazar finally.

There was a momentary buzz in the crowd and eyes fixed on Jeshua expectantly. A couple of voices behind Jeshua made comments, though the detail was lost in the crowd. Then there was quiet. For those in the crowd who hoped Jeshua was *messiah* here was a moment when he could call for a revolt against the Romans. Was he about to echo the Maccabees' call for rebellion?

Jeshua looked at him and paused while the crowd quietened. Eleazar wondered if he was pausing for thought or for dramatic effect.

'You hypocrites,' Jeshua laughed suddenly, breaking the tension as dramatically as Eleazar had created it. Jeshua looked intently at Eleazar. 'Why are you trying to trap me?' Jeshua looked Eleazar in the eye and held out his hand. 'Someone bring me a denarius. Let me look at it.' Then Jeshua looked around the crowd as several people dug frantically in purses to find a coin. Perhaps they could one day tell their grandchildren about their own unique part in the story of Jeshua's confrontation with the Temple. A young man almost threw himself forward to be the first with a coin.

As if he hasn't seen a denarius before, thought Eleazar, having locked his face to betray nothing. How do I hire this man? He is *so* good.

Jeshua thanked the man and then examined the face of the coin closely for several seconds. The crowd held their breath. Then he turned it over and examined the other side too. The tension built even more. Finally he looked up and glanced around the crowd before looking at the lawyers ahead of him.

'Whose portrait is this on the coin?' he asked Eleazar. 'and whose inscription?'

'Caesar's', replied Eleazar.

'Then give to Caesar what is Caesar's,' he announced in a loud voice, then added: 'and to God what is God's.'

There was a moment of silence. Then a burst of laughter came from someone at the back of the crowd. Then another man laughed too, on Jeshua's right, and started to applaud. Jeshua caught his eye and smiled as that man whispered to someone on his left. As more people saw the significance there was more laughter and applause. Jeshua nodded to the crowd around him, smiling all the more. The lawyers stood still so that they gave nothing away.

Jeshua handed the coin back and thanked the man again before starting towards the gate. The man bowed and applauded too. Jeshua nodded politely to Eleazar as he moved past him. Eleazar just stood motionless.

CHAPTER 31

Jerusalem, the High Priest's office, the Temple,
Wednesday afternoon

Joseph was in the office with Annas when Eleazar returned looking thoughtful.

'Did Jeshua reject paying taxes to Rome?' asked Joseph. 'Annas explained what you had in mind. The stir in the crowd suggested some excitement?'

'He answered the question and he didn't answer it,' replied Eleazar, enigmatically.

'What?' said Annas. 'I thought he could only go one way or another.'

'That's what I thought too,' admitted Eleazar. 'Jeshua said: "Give to Caesar what is Caesar's and to God what is God's."' The High Priests looked at each other. Then Joseph laughed softly.

'Oh, I see!' he said. 'Oh, that is very clever of him.'

'Sorry, but am I missing something?' Annas looked at Joseph. Joseph looked back at Eleazar.

'The crowd saw the significance too?' he asked.

'They did,' nodded Eleazar.

'Jeshua effectively told us that we had better pay Caesar as Caesar deserves,' Joseph explained to Annas. 'Remember Mattathias' words as he died, in the histories of the

Maccabees revolt? "Pay back the gentiles in full[31]". And Judah the Galilean[32] called for resistance to Roman taxes, saying they were a form of slavery too, you'll recall.'

The significance hit Annas immediately and he struck his forehead at his slowness to spot it. 'Oh I see, of course I see. Pay back Caesar not least for all the Hebrew blood he has spilled.' He shook his head. 'Every Hebrew in the place would have understood what he meant.'

'Exactly.' said Eleazar, glumly. 'He could only answer yes or no and managed to answer both ways at once. All the Hebrews would have heard that as a call to revolution. Any Romans would have heard a request for obedience.'

'"Give to God what is God's" is significant too,' Annas quoted from a psalm: '"Give to God, you families of peoples, give to God glory and power"[33].'

'So we agree with Jeshua about something then,' said Joseph with a scowl. 'What he said today will be all over Jerusalem by nightfall. But I think the revolution *Jeshua* the Galilean has in mind is completely different from the one *Judah* the Galilean had in his mind. Or from the revolutionary intentions of the Maccabees.' He looked pointedly at each of them. 'His brand of giving God the glory could destroy us all unless we stop him. Either that, or the Lord Almighty is doing something very new and we are missing it completely.'

CHAPTER 32

Mount of Olives, Wednesday, early evening

It was nearly dusk as Eleazar watched Jeshua thank the family he had just visited and walk away alone from the camp they had established in the olive grove near the top of the Mount of Olives beside the road to Bethanya. He had seen the other disciples leave earlier, while Jeshua stayed to enjoy some food, drink and a short but earnest conversation with the pilgrims. The rabbi joined the road and turned towards Bethanya. As he did so Eleazar stepped into his path about thirty paces ahead.

'Brother!' said Jeshua, as he stopped a few paces short of Eleazar and smiled. 'It must be my good fortune that we meet again.'

'Excuse me confronting you like this, Rabbi,' began Eleazar. 'Have you time to speak?'

'What would you like to discuss?' Jeshua asked, 'You're alone so I suspect you are not trying to ensnare me. Will this be on your own account?'

'My own account?' Eleazar laughed. 'I suppose so. Might you bill me later?'

'Not how I work,' replied Jeshua.

'My name is Eleazar, son of Daniel, I am a lawyer in Jerusalem. Incidentally, you could be a brilliant advocate and I'd be happy to take you as a pupil.'

'Very kind of you to say so, Eleazar. So what would you like to discuss?'

'Well, you interest me,' began the lawyer. 'If I were you I would have stayed in Galilee because I would know that no one of any substance in Jerusalem would follow me. So what did you hope to achieve by coming here?' Jeshua looked at him silently. Eleazar frowned at the silence and continued: 'You know things are actually pretty black for you at the moment. You could be tried for sedition and there is a compelling case.'

Eleazar knew he was bluffing and Jeshua remained calm, on the outside at least.

'But I could help you,' continued Eleazar. 'We don't want any more Hebrews to be crucified. If I could go to the High Priest with some sort of confession, and your repentance of course, it's possible that you might be able to safely return to Galilee.'

'And which sins should I be confessing?' Jeshua chuckled, 'and repenting from?'

'You need me to tell you?' Eleazar asked with a tone of incredulity. 'You've been performing conjuring tricks to deceive the people of God! If they weren't tricks, then you're a sorcerer. You know the law well enough to know that either carries a death sentence. If that's not enough you're claiming to forgive sins. Even the High Priest can only accept the people's sacrifices to God and pronounce God's forgiveness. You and I both know that only God can actually forgive sins. That makes you guilty of blasphemy and that carries a death sentence too. God's law, the same law I have heard you say you support, demands your execution on three separate counts. You choose which one you want to confess first.'

Eleazar leaned against a tree behind him, crossed his

arms and looked Jeshua in the eye waiting for an answer. The next to speak loses, thought Eleazar.

Jeshua clearly saw here was nothing to gain from talking and said nothing. Eleazar changed tack, accepting that his first approach hadn't worked.

'I can't see how you ever thought you would make a difference. Look at your credentials. You have the charisma of a prophet, you speak well and you're brilliant with a crowd. Hence my offer to train you, which I meant. You've got a good brain for advocacy.' Jeshua smiled at this and Eleazar, of course, noticed.

'But your lifestyle completely undermines you,' Eleazar continued. 'I think that was your main mistake. You scandalise everyone.' Eleazar paused and waited wondering if the rabbi actually appreciated someone being honest and direct.

'Would you like to suggest which parts of my lifestyle I should change?' Jeshua asked.

Eleazar laughed coldly: 'Where do I begin? Let us assume that nothing untoward is happening with any of the men you are with but you can see how even that looks in some quarters, can't you? A thirty-year-old taking married men from their wives, and young men from their parents?' Eleazar paused but Jeshua just looked impassively at him and said nothing.

Eleazar went on: 'The less kindly among us could point at your lineage. We all know the Messiah's lineage. It's not hard to check whether you're from the line of David. But there's a story that your mother was impregnated by the Holy Spirit of God and that that's why you call the Lord "Father". Did you make that up or did she? Was it for her benefit or yours? But surely that just draws attention to the nature of your birth. And maybe to your mother's moral standards too.' Surprised to see pain in Jeshua's eyes at this attack on his mother, Eleazar turned the knife in the wound.

'Your father married her, we hear. So were you the result of premature lust? Did your father do the decent thing? A generous thing, admittedly. Or was your mother raped by one of the occupiers? Did you ever know for sure that Joseph was your father? Either way, not your fault is it? Perhaps you're part-gentile?' Eleazar guessed that, however impassive Jeshua appeared, he must be being hurt so he continued the attack.

'Didn't you learn from your childhood that you needed to be more careful in your dealings with women? Lazarus of Bethanya is a good man but you and I both know that his family circumstances are, shall we say, unusual. His sisters are both unmarried. If they are ever to find good husbands, neither need any hint of an illegitimate romance with an itinerant preacher, do they?'

'You threaten his sisters' marriage prospects and you take their money and their hospitality too. Is that because you abandoned your responsibilities to your family in Nazareth? Why did you choose a life on the road and the adulation of the crowds instead of earning a proper living by taking on your father's business when he died? You must have so disappointed your family. Does your mother still support you, in spite of the damage you've done?'

CHAPTER 33

Eleazar paused but he got nothing more than an impassive stare from Jeshua. He was interested to see how Jeshua was reacting to hearing what was being said behind his back. Cheering crowds were always nice but Eleazar made his living from exploiting the observations and feelings of the people on the edge of those crowds. Had Jeshua heard their reactions before, Eleazar wondered.

'There's at least one more woman though, isn't there?' Eleazar went on. 'Isn't your closest from Galilee too, Magdala? Another Mary? Possessed by demons, wasn't she? Her family have disowned her and so she travels with you.'

'Are you following your father Joseph's example by caring for the needy? Looking after a poor woman who has to accept any shelter she can? On cold nights on the road it must be good to have someone to curl up with. She's pretty isn't she? Is she your concubine? Relief when the frustrations of life get too much but without the cost of being a responsible Hebrew husband?' Jeshua had looked Eleazar in the eye throughout. Finally he spoke.

'"For I was envious of the arrogant;"' Jeshua began, '"I saw the prosperity of the wicked. For they have no pain, their bodies are sleek and sound. They are not troubled as others are, they are not plagued like other people. Therefore pride is their necklace and violence covers them like a garment …"'

Eleazar cut him off: 'Are you saying we in the Temple are arrogant?'

'That part of the psalm finishes: "they scoff and speak with malice, loftily they threaten oppression."' Jeshua looked Eleazar straight in the eye as he continued, 'Have you not been "loftily threatening oppression"? Or are you just being a lawyer berating a witness?'

Being compared with the wicked changed Eleazar's approach. He paused in thought, then smiled back at Jeshua. The tone of malice subsided.

'So is there no truth in what the Pharisees say about your lifestyle?' he asked.

'Not the bits you mentioned so far, no,' replied Jeshua. 'I do live on the road with some of my disciples. Some are married. Some are young. Some are women, some having been put away by husbands. I don't need to tell you how hard it is for a woman to survive if she is put away, instead of being given a proper divorce. Many prophets, ones that you and I both honour, lived as I do now. You talk of marriage: I cannot follow my calling and be married. That really would be irresponsible. You threaten to charge me? If any of the gossip was true you would arraign me for sorcery, adultery and a variety of other offences, wouldn't you?' Jeshua paused. Eleazar could see that Jeshua knew that there was no evidence against him.

'If the Pharisees, or anyone else for that matter, wish to think badly of me then doesn't that comment on the state of their hearts?' asked Jeshua.

'Can I ask about the wonders you perform, since you mentioned them?' asked Eleazar.

'I didn't mention them,' Jeshua pointed out. 'You mentioned sorcery, which I do not practice. The signs of the Kingdom are from the Father in heaven. They are completely different.'

'As you wish,' Eleazar acknowledged the correction. 'May I ask about them anyway? Why not just do more signs, if you are from God? Isn't it important that you guarantee the outcome God wants, if you can? If you are from God, surely you have the power to create any outcome God wants. Why not come into the Temple and perform some great sign? Then you'll be believed, won't you?'

'We have the law and the prophets,' replied Jeshua. 'The city is full of people here to acknowledge a mighty rescue by God. To celebrate our people's exodus to this land. The Hebrew people are a testimony to that. Neither you, nor I, would be here, but for the Lord. Do you really need *more* signs?'

'Well, we don't,' said Eleazar, 'but common people need simple messages.'

'When I was in Galilee my disciples and I fed a whole crowd of "common people". You might use the word "miraculously". How much simpler a sign could that be? Yet those same people came to me afterwards asking if I could bring bread from heaven like Moses did. There are none so blind as those who refuse to see. My cousin John, the Baptist, sent some of his disciples to ask me whether I was the anointed one he was waiting for. I told him that the blind see and the lame walk.'

'But doesn't that make my point,' said Eleazar. 'Common people aren't capable of seeing things for themselves. That's why it's a waste of time educating them. They need to be given simple steps to obey. They have to be controlled. Ordinary folk can't think difficult things out for themselves. That's what the power of religion is all about. Without it there is no social control.'

'Oh? Is God's Kingdom about social control then?' asked Jeshua.

'What else? Why did Moses give us the law if it isn't

about control?' replied Eleazar. 'Leaving ordinary folk to find their own relationship with God is a recipe for anarchy. If anarchy is what you're preaching, then you really are dangerous. You can make people obey God. If you won't, then we have to do it.' Eleazar was emphatic: 'Your way is a danger to us.'

'Why is that?' asked Jeshua.

'Because you are opening the Kingdom to unworthy people.' Eleazar sounded incredulous at Jeshua' naivety. 'Sick people, cursed people, They're sinners! That's why they're cursed with sickness! You even told everyone in the Temple that prostitutes will come to the Kingdom before priests! We have laws for people to follow if they want to get into the Kingdom. We even let gentiles in, if they do what is needed to qualify. Why should anyone keep the law to qualify for God's Kingdom if people who don't are admitted anyway?'

'Didn't King David write that God blesses people whose sins and evil deeds are forgiven and forgotten[34]?' asked Jeshua.

'Yes, David did,' agreed Eleazar, warily.

'So was our ancestor Abraham blessed with forgiveness before or after he was circumcised?'

'Before Abraham was circumcised, I suppose,' Eleazar could see where Jeshua was taking this too but the answer was unavoidable.

'Exactly,' said Jeshua. 'Are you a Hebrew because you were born a Hebrew? A descendant of Abraham?'

Eleazar thought for a second, wondering where this question was going. 'Yes, I was born a Hebrew.'

'And will you ever *not* be born a Hebrew?'

'Of course I will *always* be born a Hebrew,' he replied sarcastically, 'No one changes what they were born as.'

'So then you keep the law because you're a Hebrew, don't you?'

'Yes, of course.'

'And Abraham was accepted by God because Abraham had faith in God,' Jeshua said. 'He was blessed with forgiveness because of that faith. He was then circumcised as a sign of that faith. You don't keep the law *in order* to become a Hebrew do you? You are a member of God's people whether you keep the law or not, aren't you?'

Eleazar couldn't fault Jeshua's logic and stayed silent.

'So you agree you keep the law *because* you are a devout Hebrew already,' Jeshua continued. 'Sinners and gentiles are God's people too. They may have become alienated from God but if they turn back to God, as Abraham did, they can be at peace with God, as Abraham was. I just encourage them to act like they are the people of God, the same way I encourage you to act like one of the people of God.' Eleazar stayed silent this time too.

'And when you sin you are still a member of God's people, aren't you?' Jeshua smiled, 'Just like the sinners you despise.' Eleazar suddenly sensed Jeshua was fighting back. 'The last time I was in Jerusalem the Pharisees brought a woman to me. She had been caught having sex with someone else's husband[35]. Have you heard the story?'

Eleazar nodded: as it happened he had been in the crowd. Bringing the woman to Jeshua had been a trap: to see if he would condemn her to be stoned to death, as Mosaic law demanded. Jeshua had not endeared himself to the Pharisees by suggesting that the sinless among them should throw the first stone at her. Needless to say none of them were sinless enough to throw that first stone. Eleazar had been busy on his way elsewhere and, with no stoning to watch, he had gone about his business. Jeshua concluded:

'The reason no one threw a stone at her was because all those righteous Hebrews in the crowd knew they were sinners just like her.'

Eleazar was speechless, his mouth was open but no words came from it. He couldn't see a flaw in Jeshua's argument but it ran counter to everything he had accepted since birth. He brushed some imaginary dust from his robe and walked past Jeshua and towards Jerusalem. Then he turned and looked back at Jeshua.

'I'm sorry but I have to leave or I will be late.' In a subdued but venomous voice he continued: 'Remember what I've said. You're a danger to everything we stand for. If you come into Jerusalem over Passover, we'll meet again.'

CHAPTER 34

Jerusalem, Eleazar's house, Wednesday evening

Eleazar had quickly bathed and changed after walking back from the Mount of Olives. He had been deep in thought, having seen Jeshua's public style and now having met the man alone. Jeshua, he had decided, was certainly trying to change their religion beyond all recognition.

He couldn't decide what the Temple's next move should be so he focused on something else and allowed his mind to mull things over. First thing tomorrow he was in front of Pilate for young Benjamin, though he doubted he could help Barabbas or the other two. He checked his appearance in the mirror and, satisfied, headed out into the courtyard where a litter was waiting for him. He was surprised to see Reuben there too.

'Reuben! Good evening. You're still on a case?'

'It's about the Galileans. Benjamin's uncle Amos, the garrulous one from Tiberias, has just introduced me to Jeshua's treasurer. They were in the Temple this afternoon and the treasurer wants to meet you.'

'Jeshua's treasurer?' Eleazar brightened at the thought that serendipity might be about to intervene.

'Yes,' said Reuben with a smile. 'One of the Twelve, his inner circle.'

'Well, that is a positive development.'

'Better than that,' smiled Reuben, 'He was upset at today's breakdown between his rabbi and the Temple. He's wondering whether he has misjudged his rabbi. Jeshua's rebellion against Rome won't succeed without an alliance with the Temple and he thinks we're the people to get Jeshua to the High Priest. He wants me to set up a private meeting for Jeshua with the Temple leaders. Then he can prove he's *messiah* and take on the Romans.'.

'Funnily enough,' Eleazar laughed, 'I have just had a private discussion with Jeshua of Nazareth. I don't think Jeshua has anything like that in mind.' He thought for a few moments. 'No matter, there's an opportunity here for us anyway. Who is this treasurer? Another Galilean?'

'He's a Judean actually, a man called Judah Iscariot, but he has been with Jeshua since the early days.'

'I'm sure the High Priest will be delighted if we can get Jeshua to him but probably not the way this Judah Iscariot might think. Let's think about this for a moment.' It had been a long day and Eleazar still had a dinner to go to and an early start in the morning. He took a deep breath and cleared his head. 'How did you leave things with them?'

'I brought Iscariot here earlier but you were away. I guessed that you would want to meet him tonight,' answered Reuben, 'so I've asked Iscariot to meet me here four hours after sunset.'

'Very good, Reuben,' smiled Eleazar, scratching his head as he thought. 'Are you busy tonight?'

'At home,' he replied.

'Can you work tonight, please?'

'They'll cope without me,' smiled Reuben.

'Good, but please apologise to your wife for me,' said Eleazar. 'I can't break this dinner engagement tonight so could you get to the Temple? Find Jonathan the Guard

Captain. Tell him what you've just told me and ask him to meet me here about half an hour before you meet Iscariot. Then Jonathan and I can work out how we want to use this when you introduce us. Meanwhile, what's this chap like?'

'He only knows you by reputation but I think his family come from the same southern part of Judah as yours. He was quite impressed that this house was in the exclusive district on the west side of Jerusalem. I pointed out that you live not far from the Herodian and Hasmonean Palaces and that Joseph the High Priest is a near neighbour.'

'Easily impressed by wealth, then?' asked Eleazar.

'A bit of a zealot too,' nodded Reuben. 'He was quite scathing about the decadent, Roman-style decorations that less observant Hebrews than you acquire for their houses. He noted your possessions and your exquisite taste but that you have no human figures nor images of birds or animals. You're obviously a very devout man.'

'He's obviously a fine judge of character then,' laughed Eleazar. 'Do you think he could be particularly tempted by feeling important?'

'Definitely,' said Reuben. 'Perhaps more than most. He's a Judean and I think he looks down on the Galileans around his rabbi.'

CHAPTER 35

Four hours later Eleazar returned, having left a dinner as early as he could politely do so. As he briskly entered his house he nodded at the news that Jonathan had arrived a few minutes earlier. Reuben and Judah Iscariot had arrived too. The servants had already shown them into separate reception rooms and they had been served some refreshments. Eleazar needed to see Jonathan first.

'Jonathan, welcome,' said Eleazar, embracing him, 'Thanks for coming at short notice. I think I have a plan to get Jeshua executed for sedition before Passover. Has Reuben told you we have suddenly acquired a contact amongst Jeshua's inner circle of disciples? Even better, he wants me to introduce his rabbi to you and the High Priest. I met Jeshua this afternoon privately too by the way, on the Mount of Olives, Clearly this disciple doesn't know that.'

Jonathan nodded: 'Yes, Reuben told me. This Iscariot fellow thinks he is now a major power broker. So what do you have in mind?'

'Well, in order to get Jeshua arrested we need to find a time when we can meet him along with enough muscle to arrest him. Then we need to get him before Pilate with a convincing case to get him to execute Jeshua with Barabbas and the others on Friday. That's if I can't get them all off tomorrow.'

'Is there any hope for those four, incidentally?' asked Jonathan.

'Not much, I'm afraid,' Eleazar shook his head sadly. 'I think the boy was in the wrong place at the wrong time. Funnily enough, I think the Romans accept that but apparently Barabbas is refusing to say he's innocent. Not that anyone's been able to see Barabbas, of course.'

'Really?'

'They're denying him representation because he's guilty. Well, that's not what they're saying but it's pretty obvious. I can't see why they are still pursuing the case against the boy though, so I hope I can get him acquitted, at least. The others, if we are honest, are guilty as charged and we all know it.'

'Well, let's not abandon hope for them, eh? Meanwhile Jeshua has quite a following among the great and good of Jerusalem too,' Jonathan rubbed his beard thoughtfully. 'Can he be silenced without causing problems among the Sanhedrin? Do we bring a formal case there too?'

'An interesting question,' said Eleazar smugly. 'We may think Jeshua has broken God's laws but why do we need to formally try him in front of the Sanhedrin? We're not going to execute him are we?' Jonathan looked puzzled so he went on:

'The Romans will execute him for sedition. He's not a Roman citizen, so the Romans can try him summarily and execute him on Friday morning when they're planning to execute Barabbas and his men. I'll talk to my contacts in Pilate's office tomorrow so they know he's coming. So our aim with this man now is to get him to agree to bring his rabbi somewhere where we can arrest him tomorrow. We'll dress that up for now as a discreet place to meet representatives of the High Priest.'

'Well, we'll have to move fast tomorrow then,' said

Jonathan. 'When we know the details, I'll arrange things as early as possible tomorrow. We also need to get him to make sure he doesn't tip off Jeshua and the other disciples before the meeting.'

'Don't worry. I already have an idea about that too.'

CHAPTER 36

'Reuben, how good of you to come,' said Eleazar as he and Jonathan entered the room where Judah had been waiting with Reuben. Then he held his hands out and embraced Judah. 'Welcome! I am so glad to meet you and I am so sorry for the delay. When I heard you would come tonight I wanted get back as early as possible but, as I'm sure you know, politeness makes its demands. I am very grateful that you were willing to wait until this hour.' Judah blushed slightly and bowed in response.

'I gather you're called Iscariot?' Eleazar continued. 'That name suggests you're from Kerioth, near my own birthplace in Telem.'

Eleazar guessed Judah would be delighted to learn that both their families came from the southern villages, near the border with Edom, which had been given to the tribe of Judah after Israel's return from Egypt.

'That's right, Sir.' Judah smiled. 'From Kerioth.'

'This is Jonathan, Captain of the Temple Guard,' said Eleazar. 'He answers to the High Priest and is also a key point of contact with the Romans. That gives us some insights as to their intentions.'

The two men embraced formally too. 'You are a disciple of Jeshua then?' asked Jonathan.

'Yes, Sir,' answered Judah 'I understand from Reuben that the Temple would like to make discreet contact with my master?'

'Well, so far the public contact has been rather impolite and occasionally violent,' said Jonathan, 'We would like to know why, when Jeshua's people are oppressed by the pagan Romans, he attacks the Temple and causes trouble for the High Priest?'

'Today was not designed to be an attack on the Temple itself, as I understand it,' said Judah, 'just an image of…' but he was cut off by Jonathan.

'It doesn't matter what it was an image of. It's nearly Passover. Thousands of pilgrims are coming to get their animals sacrificed. The Temple is packed. The pilgrims already have their patience tested by the queues. No one needs hours of extra delays because someone wants to make a point, however well-intentioned he might be.'

'I'm sorry, Judah,' Eleazar intervened in a softer tone, 'but you see how difficult Jeshua is making things for the High Priest, don't you? So far Jeshua won't even tell us whose authority he claims to have.'

'I can't speak for my master's authority,' said Iscariot, 'but I'm here to help set up a meeting so that he can explain everything to you.'

'Well, that would be a very useful start,' agreed Eleazar. 'Jeshua has a following among the people, some of whom seem to think he might be the anointed one of God. Most senior people here in Jerusalem are reserving judgement although I do have friends who have been impressed. A colleague of mine was particularly struck by his story about the Samaritan who helped a traveller attacked in the Wadi Qelt. Do you know the story? The Levite passed by the victim of the robbers?'

'Jeshua has told the story a few times,' Judah smiled and nodded.

'Well, as a result of talking to Rabbi Jeshua about it, my colleague is now one of his most passionate supporters. He started quite a radical work supporting victims of crime.

That's one of the perks of being rich and righteous, one might say.' He and Jonathan smiled together.

'Sir,' said Judah, 'if you had seen what we have seen then I am sure you too would come to the same conclusion as your colleague. If the Temple is allowed to assess Jeshua's claims fairly, it may also conclude that he has the Lord's authority.'

'But that,' said Eleazar, pouring himself a drink while he spoke, 'is our problem. How are we to recognise him? The High Priest is a senior leader of Israel. Jeshua has done nothing but undermine his authority in the Temple and disrupt good order. Are we surprised that the High Priest is having trouble deciding whether Jeshua is anything but a charlatan?'

'If I may add, Eleazar,' interposed Jonathan, 'Jeshua isn't helping with our relations with the Romans either. Huge crowds moving around the country without planning or control make the Romans nervous so soon after the recent uprising. Even if Jeshua isn't actually stirring up trouble, with Passover close and lots of pilgrims about, things could get out of hand by accident. I doubt he wants innocent blood on his hands.'

'Hence my coming here tonight,' answered Judah. 'I've always advised Jeshua to establish his credentials with the High Priest. How can we proceed?' Eleazar and Jonathan looked at each other for a moment.

'Knowing where he is would help. Could you bring him to us?'

'He'll probably be in the Temple tomorrow,' suggested Judah.

'We gathered that, but a big meeting in the Temple might be misunderstood,' said Eleazar. 'Somewhere more discreet, perhaps?'

'Does Jeshua plan armed action against the Romans?' asked Jonathan.

There was a pause. Eleazar wondered if Judah had any idea what Jeshua's long-term plans were, now or after the Passover. Perhaps there were none.

'What is the role of *messiah* other than to restore the Kingdom of Israel and to sit on the throne of David?' Judah replied after the pause and immediately smiled since it said everything about Jeshua's plan but shared nothing. Eleazar and Jonathan looked at each other.

'We need to speak to Jeshua with all speed,' said Eleazar, 'so that we can organise ourselves appropriately. When *messiah* comes the Temple will be ready to do its part. So could we meet him tomorrow?'

'There will be a Passover feast in Jerusalem tomorrow night,' said Judah. 'From there he will probably go to Gethsemane to pray, as he often does, on his way back to Bethanya. Can it wait until after dark?' Jonathan and Eleazar looked at each other. Eleazar nodded to Jonathan.

'Gethsemane would be ideal,' said Jonathan. 'Will you let us know when we can come and meet him?'

'Why don't I come here when the meal finishes?' offered Judah.

'That would be perfect. Is that alright with you, Eleazar?' Eleazar nodded his approval again, then added:

'I think it is also essential that no one outside this room knows of these discussions, apart from the High Priest. Jonathan and I will personally brief him in the morning. Do we all agree?'

'Iscariot,' Jonathan added. 'This will sound rather strange but will you trust me on this? I am an expert on security after all. It looks to us as though Jeshua, for all his brilliance as a leader, is not being well advised by most of the people around him, apart from yourself perhaps. No one else is thinking about his relationship with the High Priest, are they?' He glanced at Eleazar, who smiled. 'Otherwise I suspect they would have already made approaches to us here, wouldn't they?'

'I suppose that's right,' agreed Judah. 'I hadn't looked at it like that before.'

'You are doing your job for Jeshua with skill and loyalty,' Jonathan assured him. 'Maybe the others are letting him down?'

'Well, I wouldn't want to be unfair,' started Judah.

'Of course not and nor would we. But this is now a dangerous situation for Jeshua. I suggest you tell no one about this discussion, not even Jeshua himself, in case he lets slip to someone less aware of the dangers than yourself. What if the Romans get to hear?'

'Ah! I see what you mean.' Judah agreed conspiratorially. 'I'll keep it to myself until tomorrow night.'

'Good,' said Jonathan. 'We'll be ready to go with you to Gethsemane whenever you suggest. But if the word gets out before Jeshua can tell us his plans there could be a disaster. It could cost lots of Hebrew lives for no purpose.'

'You can rely on me,' Judah assured them. 'No one will know. I think even Jeshua will be surprised.'

'I'm sure he will be,' Eleazar chuckled. 'I know we can rely on a loyal Judean. Thank you for coming here tonight. One final thing; I know you are doing this for the glory of Israel and the Lord, so will you accept a token of our support.' He took a purse from within his robes and offered it to Judah. 'Thirty silver pieces should help matters along.' Judah was effusive with his thanks.

Reuben saw that Eleazar wanted the meeting finished, so he took Judah by the arm: 'Judah, come and stay as my guest tonight.' As Reuben indicated the door, Judah kissed Eleazar on both cheeks as a farewell. 'Until tomorrow then,' Judah offered a similar farewell to Jonathan and departed with Reuben.

CHAPTER 37

The two men smiled at each other with satisfaction. Eleazar called for a slave who was waiting just outside the door and asked him for washing bowls.

'That went rather well,' said Eleazar.

'Why the money though?' asked Jonathan

'Iscariot may keep his mouth shut because he thinks his colleagues will misadvise Jeshua,' smiled Eleazar. 'Or he might want to brag that he's got contacts with us and they haven't. I think he'll probably want at least some of the money for himself. To keep quiet about the money, he'll have to keep quiet about meeting us.'

When the slaves brought the bowls of water, both men washed their faces and beards, then dried themselves. 'Live with the Romans long enough and you realise how little most Jerusalemites bath,' commented Eleazar as his slave took away his bowl.

Jonathan laughed. 'That man has clearly been in the desert too long.' He passed his towel back to the slave serving him, who bowed and left as well.

'Well, we'll have to move fast tomorrow night,' said Jonathan, rubbing his beard thoughtfully. 'I'll organise people as early as possible. We'd better brief the Romans tomorrow too. They prefer to think they're in control.'

'Good. Can we see Annas and make sure he's content with the plan?' asked Eleazar. 'I'm in the Temple all morning once I've spoken for the boy. Send for me when you know when Annas wants to see us. Are you enjoying working with him by the way?'

'He's a sharp thinker,' replied Jonathan. 'Jeshua couldn't have come here at a worse time though, so it's good to have someone like him who knows the High Priest's work but isn't tied up with the detail of actually leading all the Passover sacraments. This would all be much more of a problem, given Joseph's immersion in religious ceremony.'

PART FIVE

THURSDAY BEFORE PASSOVER

CHAPTER 38

Temple Mount, High Priest's office, Thursday morning

'Well done, Eleazar. Another acquittal!' said Annas as he welcomed Eleazar into the office. 'The talk was that the boy would be executed too.'

'Thank you,' smiled Eleazar modestly. 'I'm not sure it was my advocacy skills this time though. I think the whole thing was for show.'

'What do you mean?' asked Annas. 'I know we all secretly wanted the uprising to succeed but the three of them were guilty of sedition against the Romans, weren't they?'

'Yes, and the boy was innocent and justice was seen to be done,' agreed Eleazar.

'So how was it a show then?'

'I think the Romans wanted to show Barabbas is a nasty murderer who would have sacrificed an innocent for his own purposes. The Empire is shown to be a law-abiding government defending innocent citizens against murderous rebels.'

'You mean they knew the boy was innocent all along and just kept him in prison to then acquit him anyway? Just to discredit Barabbas and the zealots?'

'Exactly,' said Eleazar. 'Pilate hopes to split the zealots

away from the rest of the Judean people.'

'Well, most people will forget it all pretty soon anyway, I suspect. At least there won't be a riot about an innocent boy's death.' Annas scratched his head and looked across the city from the High Priest's offices. 'So let's move on, we still have Jeshua to deal with.' Jonathan had already recounted the events of the meeting with Jeshua's disciple as they waited for Eleazar to arrive. 'It sounds like this Iscariot is driven by a sense of his own self-importance,' suggested Annas, 'and he has deluded himself into thinking that Jeshua is *messiah*. Is that right?'

'That's our assessment,' said Eleazar. Jonathan nodded his agreement.

'Well then. I see no point in reminding him how many would-be *messiahs* there have been in recent years,' Annas continued. 'Given Antipas' own ambitions in that regard one might say competitors. Jeshua is more memorable than most, perhaps even in his own league but *messiah* isn't recognised just for distinction or charisma. Iscariot's naivety isn't our problem either, nor is it our task to set him straight. How will things progress tonight, Jonathan? Will Iscariot be suspicious about a party of guards?'

'Eleazar is organising two council members to accompany us. It's night so there'll be nothing unusual about me taking some bodyguards and torchbearers.'

'Will you recognise him in the dark?' asked Annas.

'Iscariot will confirm which one is Jeshua,' Jonathan replied.

'Fine,' said Annas. 'Arresting him is only part of the battle and we're short on time.' He turned back from the window. 'Eleazar, are you sure we can get him executed by the Romans tomorrow?'

'Yes, if we still want him dead before Passover,' replied Eleazar.

'Jonathan?' asked Annas.

'While he's alive there a risk of trouble from his supporters,' said Jonathan. 'Look at what happened when he arrived on Sunday. There were boys shouting "Hosanna" at the Romans most of that night and that word is already becoming a call for revolution. With Jeshua actually in prison we could have even more trouble on the streets. Then there's the *siccari* and the zealots to think about. They might use unrest as a cover to settle scores. A lot of people could get killed.'

Annas thought again for a moment. 'Then Joseph is right: it's better that he dies not many.'

'Fine. I've already arranged that Pilate will try Jeshua tomorrow if he's in custody tonight,' said Eleazar. 'But can't a man take days to die once crucified?'

'That's already arranged,' Jonathan replied. 'The Romans know we want them dead before Sabbath. If necessary they'll break their legs so that they suffocate before sunset.'

'How kind of them to be so obliging!' Annas harrumphed, disgusted at the thought. All three were silent for a moment. 'It's sad but I fear there is nothing more we can do for them,' said Annas. 'You say Pilate will hear Jeshua's case tomorrow morning?'

'Yes. I've arranged a time at dawn,' Eleazar confirmed, 'Pilate will hear the case summarily. Jeshua isn't a Roman citizen so there's no need for formal written proceedings. I do have one small legal concern though.'

'Oh, yes? What's that?' asked Annas.

CHAPTER 39

'Evidence?' smiled Eleazar. 'Do we actually have *any* witnesses yet? Someone for instance who would testify that Jeshua was inciting insurrection? I doubt Judah Iscariot will testify and on this morning's form, Pilate may enjoy taking the credit for releasing the innocent.'

'Well, no,' said Annas in a rather sour tone. 'Nothing yesterday succeeded in getting him to say anything seditious. If anything he's been a model of civic loyalty: "Give Caesar what he's owed". The words themselves won't convict him. He's talked about being the "Son of Man", which sounds like it could be a messianic interpretation of the prophesy of Daniel. We could explain that to Pilate as a claim to being a king but I don't think we could put any witnesses together to support the allegation. None Pilate would believe anyway.'

'It would make life easier but I thought not,' said Eleazar.

'So what do we do?' asked Jonathan.

'At the interrogation tonight he might say something incriminating but I will assume he won't. Don't worry, that's why you hired me. We'll just revert to what the Romans call a *maiestas* charge,' said Eleazar. 'It's a charge of impugning the majesty of the Emperor. Jeshua's claims to be a king impugns the Emperor's majesty. To be honest it's a Roman legal device for convicting a troublesome innocent. Pilate knows that.'

172

'Is that really the best we can do,' Jonathan looked slightly aghast. 'Will Pilate accept it?'

'Perhaps not if we just tell him Jeshua is claiming to be a king of the Hebrews,' Eleazar smiled. 'But if we warn him that we'll tell the Emperor if he doesn't convict a dangerous rebel, then he might.'

'Why would that make him effectively pervert a capital trial?' asked Jonathan.

'Did you know Pilate was one of Sejanus' protégés? He's one of the last of Sejanus' men who hasn't been assassinated yet. Probably for no better reason than that Pilate is here, a long way away, out of sight and out of mind.' Eleazar paused to let that sink in and then continued. 'Pilate won't want the Emperor asking why he released a dangerous rebel, will he? Pilate won't like a *maiestas* case either but I think he'll prefer it to his family being killed.'

He looked at Annas and Jonathan in turn. They had understood that point so he went on: 'More positively, I am sure he knows that he's making a nice little fortune as governor here. In a few years time the whole thing will have blown over. Tiberius will die eventually and no one will remember Jeshua of Nazareth. Then Pilate can return to Rome a rich man. Would he really release a nobody and risk his own life and a wealthy future for the sake of a bit of hard evidence? Pilate? I don't think so.'

'He'll prefer to keep taking the money, you mean?' asked Annas.

'I think so and unless we find witnesses to a capital offence tonight, do we have any other choice?' asked Eleazar with an air of finality.

'I don't like it, any more than I expect Pilate will, but it sounds like it'll work,' agreed Annas. 'Can we convince our own people though? The Sanhedrin can't try a man at night, can it?'

'Well that's going to be easier actually,' replied Eleazar, 'because we aren't going to try him.'

'Aren't we?' asked Annas.

'No. A proper trial must be in daylight and that simply isn't possible. I dare not think how many rules we'd break if we tried him overnight. But the Romans are going to try him anyway. Do we actually need to try him ourselves?' Eleazar, the experienced trial lawyer, stressed that key word "try".

'Well, do we?' asked Annas slightly mystified.

'No, we just need to get him to admit, in front of reliable witnesses, to a blasphemy. We don't need to convict him of blasphemy in front of a court of law. We already know he isn't really *messiah*. We just need some reliable people to hear him say some blasphemous things. Then we can tell the Hebrew people, quite truthfully, that he publicly contravened the Law of Moses. The Romans will try him for sedition. Having got him to admit that he thinks he's *messiah*, or the Son of God, or the Son of Man, or whatever he wants to call himself, we've got everything we need.'

'So we don't need a formal verdict, then?'

'No, not in a Hebrew court. I don't need him to be convicted by the Sanhedrin to know he's a charlatan, do I? Do either of you? Does anyone else?'

'So your plan is? In summary?' asked Annas, still sounding a little confused.

'When we arrest him, we interrogate him in front of Sanhedrin members. Credible people, known to be honest and trustworthy. They can tell people that Jeshua blasphemed and that should satisfy most people. Then we hand Jeshua to the Romans to try him for sedition.' There was a pause then Annas summed up his understanding.

'Let me see if I've got the whole picture. Jonathan and his troops arrest Jeshua with help from this Iscariot. We

174

hold an enquiry to give us a range of respected leaders all of whom can convince our people that Jeshua is a blaspheming charlatan. Then we hand Jeshua over to the Romans for a capital trial for sedition. At the moment there are no witnesses. Unless someone reliable comes forward tonight we're going to rely on Pilate deciding to execute Jeshua for impugning the Emperor's dignity thereby continuing to amass his fortune as Governor. If he refuses to execute Jeshua, Pilate risks death by assassination because we'll threaten to write to Tiberius and tell him Pilate let a known rebel go free. And we're going to achieve all this, and give him time to die on a cross, before sunset tomorrow.'

'I think that's a good summary, yes,' agreed Eleazar.

'So the entire plan relies on Pilate's human greed and fear?'

'Do you know any better motivation?' asked Eleazar.

Annas looked thoughtful for a few seconds. 'In the circumstances, it's brilliant,' he smiled.

CHAPTER 40

Jerusalem, Palace of Herod, Thursday early evening

The sun was setting and Pilate was dressed for dinner as he walked into one of the reception chambers in the Herodian Palace. The rich furnishings contrasted with the armour of the Roman officers waiting there for him. The assembled company, which included Festus Maximus, rose to greet him. He acknowledged the salutes and noted that the Temple Guard Captain and Eleazar were both there too.

'Gentlemen, thank you. I am shortly to be elsewhere,' Pilate began and, noting Eleazar was also dressed for dinner, 'as is Scribe Eleazar, I suspect.' Eleazar acknowledged that with a slight smile and a nod of the head. 'It's late. So let us be brief.' Pilate sat down in a seat that had been left vacant for him with the Garrison Commander on his left. 'Please sit down. gentlemen. What can I do for you?' He arranged his robes, then looked up as one looking forward to hearing a good story. The Garrison Commander spoke as soon as the sound of moving chairs ceased:

'Prefect, the scribe and the Temple Guard commander have news of another potential armed uprising. I have put the garrison on alert as a precaution but we are not anticipating any serious trouble. The Temple Guards will arrest the leader this evening and a section of our men are available to help them as required. Your secretary has already confirmed that you would be available to hear a case of sedition first thing tomorrow.'

'Indeed,' Pilate turned to Eleazar and Jonathan. 'Well, Gentlemen! The Emperor will be delighted that his citizens are keen to preserve the integrity of the Empire against rebellious elements.' He could see Eleazar was offended by the rather ironic tone so he went on: 'Please tell me more.'

'Prefect,' Eleazar began, ignoring Pilate's sarcasm, 'you will be aware that Jeshua of Nazareth arrived in the city a few days ago.'

'I have heard the name. Is he the culprit?' asked Pilate.

'He arrived at the head of a large crowd, as you will also have been told. The manner of his arrival was symbolically very clear to Hebrew people. We have a tradition of *messiah* who will arise in the future. Actually "king" could be a good way to describe "*messiah*" in a Roman sense.' Eleazar paused emphatically looking Pilate in the eyes. 'One of our traditions is that *messiah* will enter Jerusalem to claim King David's throne and to establish an independent Hebrew state, much as existed centuries ago before the conquest of this land by the Assyrians.'

'Are you telling me Jeshua is this "*messiah* king" then?' asked Pilate.

'We acknowledge no king, other than Caesar, Prefect,' emphasised Eleazar, his tone suggesting surprise that Pilate might think the Judeans were other than entirely loyal to the Roman Emperor. 'Jeshua believes he can trace his ancestry back into the family of King David who ruled centuries ago. The manner of his arrival here a few days ago was a deliberate symbol of his intended kingship and it was not lost on local people. As you know there was a certain amount of trouble that night. It was mainly from intoxicated youths, nevertheless, given the recent insurrection, a soft approach to Jeshua would endanger the rule of law.'

'I know there was some trouble on Sunday,' said Pilate. 'Jeshua also caused trouble in the Temple yesterday. But isn't Jeshua of Nazareth just a healer? Doesn't he teach peace? Even love of our enemies?' Pilate smiled, glancing around his officers at Jeshua's evident naivety. Then Pilate's eyes narrowed. He looked back at Eleazar: 'I wasn't aware he had aspirations to government.'

'Jeshua encodes his message. This avoids him attracting Roman attention,' Eleazar replied sweeping his hand around the room. 'In our terms though, his message is clearly of the establishment of a new kingdom in Israel. So by definition Jeshua's kingdom would end the Emperor's rule here. Whatever nice, kind things he may have done for sick people, he is leading many of our people into sedition. You have doubtless heard of his phrase "let those with ears hear"?'

Pilate nodded and Eleazar continued:

'He uses it repeatedly when he tells his stories. Many of us in the Temple object to much of his teaching precisely because we can hear what he is saying. He openly declared yesterday that he would destroy the Temple itself. He is trying to overthrow our own laws as well as Rome's.' Eleazar paused to allow the point to sink in. 'The High Priest knows that religious aspects hold no interest for the Romans but the fact of sedition against Rome is clear. That of course, will interest you.'

'How are you planning to arrest him?'

'One of his supporters hopes that the Temple will join Jeshua's rebellion. He is arranging a meeting with Jeshua on the pretence of discussing that matter. Once we have confirmed his crime we will bring him to you for trial in the morning.'

'Are you proposing to try him yourself?' asked Pilate.

'Of course not, Prefect. We can all see the seriousness of the matter but we have no jurisdiction in a crime of sedition against Rome. You are the law in that regard.'

Pilate smiled at the two Hebrews: 'I know about this Galilean. My people monitor likely insurrectionists. I am familiar with your traditions and I am expert in Roman law, especially as it relates to sedition. Unless my men have recently found something I was unaware of though,' he looked at the Roman officers expectantly but they said nothing so he continued, 'then I am surprised you think Jeshua is a threat.'

'Indeed, Prefect,' Eleazar answered, 'but the nature of this crime is that it is being conducted effectively in our symbolic language. That is the only reason the Roman security services didn't pick up the threat themselves.' There was silence as Pilate looked at Eleazar without any expression.

'Isn't this all rather sudden?' said Pilate suddenly, his tone turning faintly ironic. 'Jeshua has been wandering around the Temple for days. You could have brought him to trial at some leisure but we only hear of this now? It's Thursday night! You want him tried tomorrow and presumably convicted and executed? Are you hoping,' Pilate saw a darkening in Eleazar's eyes at this word and adjusted the phrase quickly, 'or suggesting at least, that we add Jeshua to tomorrow's crucifixion of, er?' he looked at Maximus questioningly.

'Barabbas and two others, sir,' offered Maximus.

'Barabbas! Thank you, Centurion.' Pilate looked back at Eleazar.

'We have a party ready to arrest Jeshua as soon as we get word of his whereabouts,' answered Eleazar. 'We feel that there is a greater possibility of serious trouble if he isn't dealt

179

with immediately, so the Emperor's interests would be better served if he died with the other insurrectionists. None of us would benefit from Emperor Tiberius hearing there was trouble over Passover would we? Before we take action though, we felt, out of respect for you, that we should personally inform you now so that you are prepared when we bring Jeshua to you tomorrow.'

'How kind of you,' smiled Pilate. 'Are we preparing charges overnight too?

'Jeshua is not a Roman citizen,' offered the Roman Garrison Commander, 'so there is no need for written charges. You will be able to dispose of the case as you see fit tomorrow.'

'Witnesses?' Pilate asked Eleazar.

'Prefect, I can't imagine you would wish to take the risk of a potential seditionist on the loose in the Province,' replied Eleazar adding innocently, 'the Emperor certainly wouldn't want to hear of a governor releasing such a man, would he?'

Pilate looked Eleazar sharply in the eye and to his discomfort he found Eleazar returned his gaze boldly. He could see that Eleazar knew that Pilate needed nothing but positives about himself in the Emperor's ears at the moment.

'It sounds like we will see you all in the morning then,' said Pilate rather coolly. 'I appreciate the courtesy of the advanced warning. Please give the High Priest my compliments. It sounds like you may all be having a long night.' He rose to leave and his officers stood too: 'Good evening, gentlemen.'

PART FIVE

FRIDAY

CHAPTER 41

The High Priest's house, Jerusalem, Friday, the small hours

It suddenly struck Joseph that they had reached the darkest of the hours before dawn[36]. If the night was dark, he mused, it was little darker than his feelings about the increasingly fruitless interrogation that they were presently conducting. He normally considered it a failure to be out of his bed much past midnight and he was putting this whole night into that failure category. The accusations being levelled against Jeshua by different people were clearly groundless. Worse still, Jeshua could see that and was simply refusing to speak.

As planned, Jeshua's disciple, Iscariot, had led Jonathan and his men to his master. After a bit of a fracas they had arrested Jeshua. Jeshua had supposedly performed yet another miracle, healing Joseph's own slave, Malchus, who had allegedly been struck on the head by a sword in the fight[37]. On their return Malchus had confirmed that he had had his right ear injured. Sensing evidence for a quick conviction for something like attempted murder, Joseph and Eleazar had formally questioned him. A reliable man, Malchus could have made a good witness.

Malchus had accused one of Jeshua's disciples but there was little physical evidence and none against Jeshua. There was a copious amount of drying blood on his shoulder, as one might expect, but no injury. While Joseph would normally have been delighted that his slave was healthy, another apparently miraculous cure by Jeshua was, in view of the aim of the arrest, less than helpful. In any case, as Eleazar had pointed out, even with a severed ear and a culprit to accuse, one would be hard put to get a conviction, given the facts of several armed men blundering about in an unlit olive grove on a dark night.

Joseph had been intrigued by the blood. Maybe Jeshua really had healed it. More sorcery? Even if proved, it wasn't very helpful since, given the present mood in the city it might be taken as evidence of Jeshua as anointed, rather than being in a pact with Beelzebub. Pilate would just laugh if asked to consider a healing as evidence of sedition.

The interrogation had not begun until well after midnight. The main reception room in Joseph' house was full of Sanhedrin members and people who claimed to have evidence of sedition against Rome. The trial in front of Pilate was now only an hour or so away and so far there was nothing that would stand even a cursory investigation by the Governor.

Joseph rubbed his eyes as yet another Pharisee finished testifying that he had heard Jeshua say that he would destroy the Temple in three days and then rebuild it. This is going nowhere, he thought. Threats to demolish and rebuild one of the biggest buildings in the world might convince Pilate that Jeshua was completely insane. It would not convince him that Jeshua was a threat to the Roman Empire.

Eleazar had been right. They would have to construct a charge that Jeshua insulted the dignity of the Emperor. Joseph didn't think Pilate would like that either, but if he tried to dismiss it, Joseph had agreed they could threaten to tell Tiberius that Pilate was letting a dangerous criminal go.

The Emperor wouldn't waste time investigating a supposed miscarriage of justice against a labourer who wasn't even a Roman citizen. Tiberius probably would act if a protégé of the treasonous Sejanus was less than diligent about rooting out rebels.

Joseph stifled a yawn as politely as he could. He looked at Jeshua, who was sitting, apparently impassively, having hardly spoken a word all night. *We can sleep peacefully tomorrow at least,* he thought, *if we know he's a blasphemer.*

Do we know he's a blasphemer? That thought reminded Joseph of a nagging doubt he'd had about Jeshua all along. *We've assumed that messiah will come to lead us to free the ancient Hebrew lands. Yet the Lord's ways are not always our ways,* he reminded himself. *We've assumed that messiah might be like us but might God choose a complete outsider?* Joseph couldn't conceive how that could be, but what if...? His brain struggled even to engage with the question at this hour. *If Jeshua was messiah and had properly forgiven sins, then didn't that make him God in flesh? Emanuel: God is with us.* Joseph's brain suddenly raced at that thought then another came hard on its heels. *That would mean this Jeshua is either a charlatan or worse. Or everything he says he is. So are we about to kill messiah?*

He closed his eyes. *If he's not anointed we can condemn him by our own laws, even if the legal case is questionable to the Romans. If we let him go free we endanger the nation, so the end will justify the means.*

Yet this man is doing nothing to avoid his own death. If he is messiah does God need him to die? If Jeshua is Emanuel has God decided to die himself? Joseph knew that many godly Hebrews had been martyred in the past. *If we don't kill him will we be standing in God's way? So is letting Jeshua die doing God's work, even though our part will be to sacrifice an innocent?*

So perhaps it is still better that one man should die for the sake of the nation than that the whole nation should die? With a vague hope that that phrase wouldn't become his epitaph, Joseph made up his mind. Jeshua has to die.

That decision made, he realised that he had to finish this himself. He held his hand up and the room went quiet.

'How do you respond to the testimony that these men are bringing against you? Have you no answer?' Joseph asked calmly. Jeshua's silence continued.

'I put you under oath before the living God,' demanded Joseph emphatically. 'Tell us if you are the anointed one.'

'You say so,' said Jeshua, finally speaking for himself, 'and you will see the Son of Man sitting at the right hand of the Mighty One and coming with the clouds of heaven.[38]'

Joseph stood and with relief, ceremoniously tore part of his robe. 'Why do we need any witnesses? You have heard the blasphemy,' he signalled at Jonathan. 'Captain, hold him while we discuss the case.'

CHAPTER 42

Jerusalem, Palace of Herod, Friday morning, dawn

Just before dawn Pilate stirred as he became vaguely aware of logs being quietly placed onto the fire in the room ready for his and Claudia's rising. Semi-conscious, he pulled his bedding around his neck to stop the cold air from the room mixing with the warmth of his bed. He snuggled up to Claudia alongside him: body heat, silk sheets, silky skin, musky scent. She purred sleepily as he fitted snugly into her soft curves. He savoured the sensations and hardened as she gently rubbed his lap with her bottom. Passion filled him and he wondered if they could get up a bit later? He tried to remember the tasks for the day to come. Oh yes, the High Priests' would bring Jeshua to him at dawn.

He felt his stomach tighten with a sickening clench. It dispelled warmth, sleepiness, passion and any thrilling anticipation. He raised his head and glanced across at the slave who had just stood up having finished stoking the fire. Noticing that Pilate had awakened, the girl bowed in his direction and hurried from the room.

Pilate uncurled himself from Claudia and reached out for the cup of water on the table by his bed. He noted his clothes hung out around the fire, to be warm when he put them on. He took a drink, the cold water reinforcing the contrast between the warmth of their bed and the chilly air in the room. He put the cup down and then, withdrawing his hands from the outside, lay in his bed, the covers pulled up to his ears. He would have been beautifully warm apart from the chill that was concentrated in the tip of his nose. April in Jerusalem: often cold at night.

Last night he had seen the necessity of neutralising Jeshua before the festival. No one wanted the uprising to break out again. Just as bad would be violence between Jeshua's supporters and those of the Temple. The trouble at his entry into Jerusalem earlier that week had been easily contained: it had been little more than excited youngsters. Passover always attracts the serious troublemakers too. Murderous *siccari* came to Jerusalem during festivals. With the city so crowded, it was the easiest time to disappear having assassinated a target. He was holding Barabbas and the zealots captured with him. Some of their comrades might want to try to strike or even be planning to rescue their friends. Executing them before Passover reduced the possibility for trouble. That was why he had agreed that, if there was a charge to answer, the priests could bring Jeshua first thing this morning.

Jeshua isn't a Roman citizen, so there could be a spoken accusation. We can dispose of the matter quickly, he thought, before many of Jeshua's supporters realise their hero has been taken.

As the fire warmed the room, he lay in his bed thinking. He could see no crime that Jeshua had committed. This was just a *maiestas* case. So the priests must want Jeshua dead for their own reasons. Offences against the Emperor's majesty were flimsy at the best of times. Was there any real evidence of sedition? We would have already taken him if we knew of any real offence, so are we just being used as judicial executioners? Was he, Pilate, just the bumbling pagan doing the priests' dirty work so their hands appeared clean to their own people?

Somewhere, just as with the Hebrews objecting to the standards, Pilate thought there probably was a way of dealing with Jeshua without becoming the priests' puppet himself. But he didn't have the faintest idea what it was.

As his irritation grew he swung himself out of bed. He had come to Jerusalem expecting the normal round of parties, dinners and lunches to take his mind off the all-pervading smell. Instead he now had to keep the lid on a religious dispute that had the potential to turn into another insurrection. Only the gods knew where that might end.

Suddenly he knew again that feeling that all soldiers know: the only way out of this mess is through it. In a few hours it'll all be over, he decided. He couldn't remember with whom lunch was booked but he did remember thinking that it would be a good one. He yawned and shook Claudia, who rolled towards him, looking rather disappointed.

'I thought you were going to wake me up nicely,' she said, sounding disappointed. 'What's the matter?'

'If you recall, those priests are bringing your holy man to see me today,' he replied irritably. 'That's what's the matter.'

'I told you last night it wasn't a good idea to get caught up in this.' She pushed herself up onto one elbow and looked at him. 'Jeshua isn't our problem. Actually I had another dream about him last night.'

Pilate laughed: 'One minute you tell me that you want to wake up making love with me and the next you tell me you've been dreaming about Jeshua?'

She smiled back and reached out, running her fingers through his hair. 'I didn't mean I was dreaming about making love with him, silly! The point is he's done nothing that's a crime against Rome. I'd be the first to tell you to execute him if he had. Now we've both been in politics long enough to know that expediency is often the best policy, but you could end up executing an innocent man. Something about this doesn't augur well for us. You have to stay out of this.'

'Don't talk to me about bad auguries,' his voice became tetchy again. '*That's* the matter. I can't stay out of it. I'm being used and I'm buggered if I can see how to stop it.' He growled in exasperation and rubbed his shortly cropped hair fiercely with both hands. Partly it expressed his frustration. Partly it helped to wake him up. 'Come on, it's time for prayers. Then I can have a think while we eat and I get a shave.'

An hour later Pilate was still annoyed. He sat alone in one of the living rooms in the Palace munching a peach. From the duty officer's report it seemed half the Sanhedrin seemed to be outside already. The High Priest was following separately, bringing Jeshua for trial. Would the Governor please attend them outside the Palace gates? The cheek of it, Pilate thought. Where else in the whole Empire would the Roman governor be asked to leave his accommodation to attend on the subjects? Where else in the whole bloody world? This isn't going to be a good day, he decided.

Maximus entered the room and saluted. Pilate acknowledged the compliment and smiled grimly. Pilate knew Maximus had developed an interest in the culture of the Hebrews. Pilate couldn't think what was so interesting about them but then he'd never seen the attraction of watching birds or collecting sea-shells either.

'Have you ever met Jeshua, Centurion? My wife has, half my staff and anyone who's anyone in this province has. Am I the only person he's avoided so far?'

'No, Sir,' replied Maximus, sensing his superior's

discomfort, 'he's obviously decided to avoid both of us. I've heard a great deal about him too but I don't think I can tell you anything you haven't already heard from much better sources than me.'

'Actually,' said Pilate flatly, 'I'd have valued your opinion above most.' He tossed the peach stone onto a plate and wiped his mouth with a towel.

'The men have set up the *curulis* for you, Sir. There is also a scribe ready. The High Priest has just arrived with the accused.' Maximus paused, as if wondering quite how to phrase his next sentence: 'They have formally asked if the most excellent Governor would graciously attend them outside to consider the case of a wrong-doer.'

'Most excellent Governor, my arse!' exclaimed Pilate with undisguised disgust. 'Who are they fooling? They want this all done before the city wakes up. If they thought I was so "excellent" they'd be "graciously" attending us in here, instead of dragging us outside. Do they think we shit on the floors in here or something? Whose bloody empire is it anyway?'

Maximus recalled Pilate, when he was a young officer, showing similar incomprehension in the face of intransigence. He smiled. 'You're right, Sir, but it doesn't cost much to be polite to the subject peoples. We can store up a favour for the future, perhaps?'

'True,' agreed Pilate but unenthusiastically. 'Come on then.' He adjusted his white toga and strode out of the room. His temper was still a fair way from even though.

'This had better be good,' Pilate muttered as he passed the centurion and turned towards the main gate which led to the small square in front of the Palace.

CHAPTER 43

Palace of Herod, early Friday morning

Pilate and Maximus emerged from the gate and Pilate took the couple of steps onto a red rug placed in front of the doorway. On the rug was a single empty seat. The *curulis*, formed with arms and seat made from a single wooden bow shape, was the traditional seat of a Roman judge. A scribe sat slightly to the left of the *curulis*, writing materials ready in front of him on a small writing table.

In front of the seat, facing the gate, stood Joseph. To Joseph's left, Pilate recognised Annas. To their right was a dishevelled man. Pilate assumed this was Jeshua. His arms were bound with rope and there was another around his neck, by which he had obviously been led here by the four Temple Guards that stood either side and behind him. Pilate could see a black eye beginning to emerge and blood trickling from a cut to his lip.

Pilate also recognised Eleazar and Jonathan. About fifty people stood behind them all, presumably Sanhedrin members, and another twenty Temple guards besides. Slaves carrying the priests' litters stood against the walls of the building at the opposite side of the small square.

The pragmatist in Pilate understood that the innocent frequently suffered in life. As a soldier he knew the wrong people often died in wars and the right people often didn't. He knew, even if he didn't think about it very often, that most of his wealth was based on oppression but, in some indefinable way, he felt that was all different from the oppression in front of him now. Everything he'd heard suggested Jeshua was probably quite a good man. It rankled the professional soldier in him that the Temple guards seemed to have beaten a confession out of him[39].

'What charges are there against this man?' demanded Pilate, none too politely.

'If he were not a criminal we would not have brought him to you,' said Annas, waspishly. Pilate decided that Joseph had obviously delegated this prosecution to the older man. Pilate snapped.

'I have better things to do with my time. If he has committed a crime,' Pilate paused slightly to say emphatically and in a slower voice, 'against Roman law,' before he continued, 'please enlighten us. I want to know what charges you wish to put against him. If he has offended your religious laws then try him yourself. They don't matter to me.' A murmur of anger ran through the crowd in front of him. Pilate, visions of Hebrew protestors in his mind, immediately regretted that last comment. He took a deep breath and looked at Joseph, who sensed that Pilate had suffered all the indignity he was prepared to accept.

'Governor,' Joseph smiled smoothly at Pilate, who even wondered if he had noticed a slight bow from the High Priest. 'We have found this man subverting our nation[40]. He opposes the payment of taxes to Caesar and he claims to be *messiah*, a king.' That last to help the ignorant gentile, thought Pilate.

Pilate studied Jeshua for a moment. This was the sedition charge he had been briefed to expect but what was the substance? Clearly Jeshua had been upsetting the High

Priests. He'd brought part of the Temple market to a halt a couple of days ago. He'd probably breached the peace but scattering some animals around a religious shrine was hardly a capital offence. Religious disputes were personal matters as far as Rome was concerned. Was there any evidence that he had committed a crime against Rome? This charge of claiming to be a king did sound suspiciously like a *maiestas* but had he even committed an imaginary crime against the dignity of the Emperor, let alone a real one?

'Who are the witnesses to this subversion?' asked Pilate.

'We interrogated him ourselves last night and found a case of sedition to answer, among other things,' replied Joseph with a smile.

'Are you going to furnish us with the records of your enquiry?'

'This is such a simple case, Prefect, we had not planned to waste your time with the minor detail,' replied Joseph, looking Pilate in the eye. If he hadn't been on the receiving end of Joseph's guile, Pilate would have admired the nerve and skill of the High Priest. I can see why he's been in charge so long, Pilate thought briefly. Joseph continued: 'We know you have a busy day, given the festival, which is why we offered to investigate the matter overnight and bring him to you at dawn. We have no desire to interfere with your plans.'

Pilate thought for a few moments. He had no doubt there had been an enquiry last night and had no reason to doubt Joseph. Furthermore, any trouble in the future would risk him having to justify to Caesar why he hadn't accepted the High Priests' judgement in the first place. The Emperor could merely point out the crosses still lining the roads of Judea. Had Pilate been so fussy about any of those executions?

'I'm grateful for your concern, High Priest,' he replied, making sure he was not the first to break eye contact. 'You are asking for the death penalty, though. I will examine the prisoner myself.' With that he rose to his feet with all the gravitas of his office. 'Centurion,' he looked at Maximus, who took the cue and sprang to attention, 'will you bring the prisoner inside?' He stood up and walked back into the Palace acknowledging the salutes as he did so. They can all wait for a bit, he thought.

CHAPTER 44

A few minutes later he was sitting on a couch in one of the private rooms in the palace. He accepted a drink from a slave as Maximus and a lawyer entered through a pair of double doors. Maximus closed the doors behind him. Turning to the Prefect and indicating the doors they had just come through he said: 'We have the accused waiting for you, Sir.'

'Good. Listen, Centurion. You've taken an interest in a bit of Hebrew history and culture: 'Subverting our nation'? What does that mean? If they want him convicted of breaking Rome's law, why don't they just turn up with the witnesses?'

'Could be they don't have witnesses to anything we would call a crime, Sir,' Maximus replied.

'That's certainly what it sounds like to me. Have we heard him demanding an end to Roman rule or not paying duty?'

'No, Sir. In fact a day or two back in the Temple Jeshua was actually asked about taxes by some scribes. Jeshua was heard telling people to give Caesar his dues. I'm told that lawyer Eleazar was there, too.'

'Pity. A couple of witnesses would have made life easier. Well, let's see what he says for himself then.' Pilate rose and headed to the door.

Pilate entered the room with Maximus and the lawyer

to find five of his own soldiers, supposedly in charge of Jeshua, admiring the sumptuous hangings and furnishings. One was lounging on a couch, clearly the senior of the party, perhaps trying it out for comfort. As Pilate entered four sprang back from whatever they were doing and stood to attention. Jeshua stood in the middle of the room, motionless, while the fifth, a young soldier, clearly the least experienced in the group, held the rope that was around his neck. Pilate's impression of Jeshua was that he wasn't likely to be a violent man but, of all the soldiers in the room, the one actually paying attention to him would probably have been the easiest to overpower. Pilate looked at the Centurion who nodded back. Clearly, once the business at hand was out of the way, Maximus would see to it that the day would get significantly less comfortable for this little band.

Pilate regarded Jeshua quizzically for a moment. Despite the dried blood, the matted hair, beard and bruised face, Jeshua stood alert and, if not exactly proud, then with an assured bearing. He had looked silently at Pilate since the latter had entered the room. Why is it so hard to get soldiers to stand up that straight? Pilate wondered idly for a moment. The bruising was becoming even more noticeable, though. That nose looks broken and he'll have a black eye to think about soon, thought Pilate, assuming he's not nailed to a cross and concentrating on greater pains elsewhere.

'So you're the King of the Jews, then[41]?' Pilate asked.

'Did others tell you that about me? Or is that your own idea?' replied Jeshua. Pilate's jaw dropped instantly. Who is trying whom? Pilate studied Jeshua and then continued:

'It's hard not to hear about you. You seem to attract admiration and disgust about evenly. So are you a king?'

'Are we here because you think I am a king?' asked

197

Jeshua, his voice rather nasal because of the damage to his face. 'Or are we here because of what others have told you about me?'

'Am I a Hebrew?' Pilate snapped, thinking Jeshua was insulting him. 'I'm only here because your own people, your High Priests, the scribes and the rest of them have brought you to me. They are telling me that you are claiming to be their king. They want me to have you executed. What have you been doing to make them all turn against you like this?'

'Perhaps the kingdom they seek is one of this land, one of this earth. My kingdom, though, isn't a kingdom of this world,' replied Jeshua. He glanced at Maximus and there was a smile of recognition in his eye, Maximus thought. Then calmly Jeshua looked back at Pilate. 'If it were, my servants would have fought to prevent my arrest last night. But my kingdom is of another place.'

'Ah,' said Pilate: 'So you are a king then?'

'Well, you say I am a king. In fact the reason I was born was to testify to the truth. Everyone on the side of the truth listens to me.'

Pilate decided that he was going to get nowhere listening to Jeshua. Time was passing and more people would be on the street with every minute. 'Centurion, come with me please. You men,' he pointed at Jeshua and looked distastefully at the leader of the guards, 'brace yourselves up and take him back to the Temple Guards.' He then spoke to the lawyer: 'Please tell the High Priest that I will be out again shortly.' Then he looked back at Jeshua and studied him silently for a few seconds: 'Truth?' he huffed dismissively, 'What is truth?' He turned for the door followed by Maximus and the lawyer.

Pilate hadn't expected an answer but Jeshua's eyes followed them to the door. Something made Pilate turn and stare at him for a moment. He caught both calm and assurance in Jeshua's eyes. Be careful, Pontius Pilate, Jeshua's eyes seemed to say. It is as if he feels he is in control, thought Pilate, and that I'm being driven by events. Uncomfortably close to the truth too, Pilate decided. With another shake of his head Pilate turned away and left the room ahead of the others. The door swung shut behind them.

CHAPTER 45

Several minutes later when Pilate took his place on the *curulis* once more, Jeshua was already back with Jonathan and the Temple guards. Pilate spoke to Joseph: 'It doesn't sound like he's committed any crime against Roman law. Why don't you try him under your own laws if he's been offending your customs?'

'We cannot execute anyone,' Joseph replied. 'Only the Emperor's governor can do that.'

So I am just their tame executioner, thought Pilate. But there was just no way he could find Jeshua guilty of nothing. He looked at Jeshua who looked tired, dishevelled and was shivering slightly but looking him straight in the eye. I've seen that look before, thought Pilate. Is he daring me to kill him? Pilate adjusted his toga:

'Are you the King of the Jews, then?' he asked.

'Do you say that I am?' asked Jeshua in reply. Pilate's move. He inhaled deeply and looked back at Joseph:

'If you can't provide witnesses who can substantiate the accusation, I can't see any basis for this charge against this man. Do you have evidence against him?'

Eleazar spoke up for the first time: 'Prefect, he has been stirring up people all over Galilee and now he's proclaiming the coming of a new kingdom here in Judea.'

At the word 'Galilee' Pilate's heart suddenly leaped with joy[42]. Herod Antipas had jurisdiction in Galilee. He also knew that Herod wanted to meet Jeshua. Pilate could see a longer term benefit too. It could help heal a grumbling enmity that Herod and Pilate had over another massacre in the Temple courtyards that had occurred earlier in Pilate's time as governor.

Recently arrived in Judea, Pilate had been approached about inadequate water supplies to Jerusalem, especially during festivals. So Pilate had built an aqueduct to provide more water, which eased the shortage. Using Temple money though, tainted the aqueduct in Jewish eyes since the money had supposedly been sacred. Pilate felt the Jews in Jerusalem had been very unreasonable and on a subsequent visit to Jerusalem, Pilate had decided to speak to them publicly in the Temple courtyards, his soldiers in plain clothes. Surrounded by irate Jerusalemites, though, he had signalled his troops to clear the crowd and they had done so with considerable venom. Eighteen had died at the hands of his soldiers.

So Pilate saw two benefits of sending Jeshua to Herod. Herod would be pleased to see his jurisdiction acknowledged and he could sort out this case without the Romans becoming involved. Furthermore, Agrippa, Herod's nephew, was often in Rome lobbying Tiberius to replace Pilate by making him the King of Judea. Agrippa probably used any excuse to blacken Pilate in the Emperor's eyes so Herod could be a useful ally to restrict Agrippa's ambitions while it was too dangerous for Pilate to return to Rome in person.

Pilate leaned to his left and motioned to the lawyer who was positioned just inside the gate in case the Prefect needed guidance on law. He stepped up behind the *curulis* and leaned towards Pilate. Pilate inclined his head backwards and whispered into the man's ear. 'If this man has committed any crimes, he has done so mainly in Galilee, it appears. That puts him under the jurisdiction of the Tetrarch of Galilee, doesn't it?' The lawyer paused for a moment to consider the law involved, pursing his lips in thought. After several seconds the man replied:

'There is precedent for an accused to be sent from the place of arrest to the place of the alleged offence. One could easily make a case here that, since the majority of the accusations arise in Galilee, it is indeed for the Tetrarch to hear the case. The Tetrarch might also be grateful to be invited to judge the matter.'

'Excellent,' said Pilate. 'Would you draft the relevant paper to accompany the prisoner to the Tetrarch? Will you then personally present the accused to Herod with my compliments.'

'Certainly, Prefect.' The lawyer bowed slightly and smiled as he left Pilate's side. Pilate felt a twinge of pity for Jeshua at the sort of reception Herod might give him but if the whole thing was in Herod's jurisdiction it wasn't really his business. Let the Galileans sort out their own problems, he reasoned. He looked back at Jeshua, this time with a smile of one who knew the answers to all the questions he was about to ask. 'Are you a Galilean?' he asked smoothly.

'Yes. I'm from Nazareth, in Galilee,' replied Jeshua.

'You have spent most of your time in Galilee, then, including your public teaching?'

'Most of the last three years, yes.'

'And do you come to Judea often?' asked Pilate.

'No, I've only been here a few times, including visits with my family when I was a boy.'

'Very well, then.' Pilate looked at Joseph and smiled. 'High Priest, it seems, unless you have other witnesses to produce, that any seditious acts this man might have committed were committed in Galilee. Which means the Tetrarch of Galilee has jurisdiction. So I will refer the case to him.' Pilate saw the scowl on the High Priest's face which greeted this decision and he smiled inwardly, though maintaining a straight face. 'Herod, being Hebrew himself, will better appreciate the religious subtleties of this case.' With that he smiled, stood up and, with a hint of theatre, swept from his seat. His back to Joseph, he grinned at Maximus as he almost skipped into the Palace gate.

Waiting in the anteroom was Claudia Procula, who had been listening to the exchanges in the square. She greeted her husband with a hug and kissed him hard on the lips: 'Very clever!' she said.

'Well Herod is the right man to hear the case. Apart from a bit of a disturbance the other day, which they haven't raised with me, the man has done nothing here.' Pilate's morale had risen dramatically and with his spirits rising he found himself again appreciating Claudia's softness and her scent. She smiled.

'That feels like a soldier that needs a bit of tender loving care,' she whispered in his ear and squeezed his hand. 'I'll be upstairs when you've got rid of the staff.'

CHAPTER 46

Two hours later, Pilate was sitting on the *curulis* again having noticed the square in front of him was now packed. When he had left the front of the palace gate he had gone, in the space of a few minutes, from angry and frustrated to elated, having passed Jeshua to Herod Antipas. Then, just minutes ago, he had been summoned from his wife's bed, an interruption that could hardly have come at a worse moment. His ardour had cooled even more rapidly at the news that the High Priests were back with Jeshua. Herod had declined to dispose of the case.

Having been proud at how well he had avoided a confrontation with the Temple over Jeshua, Pilate was now back where he had begun. He could still see nothing in Jeshua's behaviour that deserved a death penalty but the priests were defiant and expected him to give into their pressure. Even worse, crowds were still gathering as news of Jeshua's overnight arrest was spreading. Initially made up of people accompanying the High Priests, the crowd increasingly contained Jeshua's supporters. Soon half the city would probably be hostile to him, whichever way this went. He was little comforted by the thought that he could at least choose which half.

To make things worse his soldiers couldn't tell one group of supporters from another. Scuffles had already broken out and arrests had already been made. Pilate looked at Jeshua and the High Priests standing in front of him, surrounded by Temple Guards. There was an expectant buzz coming from the crowds now jostling behind them.

In all the turmoil there was a surreal touch too. Given time, Pilate would have loved to speculate about why Herod had sent Jeshua back wearing a beautifully made, and clearly very expensive, festival robe. Was Herod just trying to humiliate Jeshua? Or was there a darker meaning? If it was a joke it was in poor taste. Such robes were the sort of thing you wore if you were seeking office or claiming a throne. Was Herod laughing at Pilate, or trying to warn him about something?

Exasperated, Pilate looked from Jeshua to the priests and then to Herod's written reply. Under most other circumstances it would have been good news. Herod was effusive with thanks. Quite apart from wanting to discuss miracles with Jeshua, he had indeed appreciated Pilate's compliment in submitting Jeshua to his jurisdiction.

If only he had also made a decision too, Pilate thought grimly to himself. He wasn't surprised that Herod sent the case back though. The Tetrarch had no more access to evidence than Pilate had. How could he have done anything but dismiss the case too? He looked again at the scowling faces that surrounded the bedraggled and beaten man in his incongruously gorgeous robe.

Pilate took a deep breath and looked at Joseph: 'High Priest, you brought me this man earlier this morning accusing him of incitement to rebellion. I examined him in your presence and found no basis for such charges in Judea. You also cannot provide any witnesses who have heard him say anything seditious. You then said most of the alleged offences were committed in Galilee, which is the jurisdiction of the Tetrarch, Herod. Herod has now examined him and has also found nothing deserving death and sent him back to us. Are you proposing that I execute an innocent man?'

Eleazar stood forward at this point. 'Prefect, I understand your regard for justice, given the gravity of the charge and sentence, but the fact remains that this man claims to be King of the Jews. Since he is using a particularly Hebrew way of proclaiming this, it is something that we find we have a duty to report to you. Since we have no King but Caesar, by definition he is committing an act of sedition, which is punishable by death. You are the judicial power representing Caesar, therefore, as good citizens of the Empire we have brought him to you. We have no other choice, and nor, it seems, do you.'

'But who witnessed this sedition? asked Pilate in an exasperated tone. 'Have you brought anyone from Galilee, where we have already established that most of these crimes are alleged to have been committed? I remind you again that the Tetrarch, who has the Emperor's jurisdiction where most of the offences you allege actually occurred, has dismissed the case. He could have passed a death sentence but refused. Why should I not release him?'

There was a ripple of applause and shouts from Jeshua's supporters. It was immediately followed by whistles and abuse from others. Another scuffle broke out and the noise halted proceedings. Out of the corner of his right eye Pilate saw Maximus deploy more troops into the crowd. This has got to stop and fast, thought Pilate, sensing his own desperation.

'High Priest,' Pilate called loudly to make himself heard over the disturbance. 'The only crime that this man has committed, it seems to me, is breaching the peace of the Temple. I will have him flogged for that and then released.'

Eleazar replied quickly without waiting for instructions from Joseph. 'Jeshua has been proclaiming himself to be a king. That is sedition. The High Priest and many of the people from our Council are here today and are witnesses to his claim to be a king. Are you doubting the word of the High Priest of Israel?' Pilate noted that Joseph nodded his support and approval of Eleazar's reply. He also noted the vociferous support from much of the crowd as well.

His troops were restraining violence in the crowd but shouting and barracking between the two factions was increasing. In desperation he made the legal play he was keeping in reserve. There was an established tradition of pardoning and releasing a convict at Passover. There were enough of Jeshua's supporters here now that it might just work. He stood up.

'People of Jerusalem and Judea,' he shouted, over the heads of the High Priests, 'to honour the long history of the Hebrew people, at Passover, I release a convicted prisoner. Shall I now release Jeshua of Nazareth and pardon him[43]?'

To his initial relief, there were shouts of approval, These though, were quickly matched by shouts of anger and derision. Seconds later Pilate saw Annas push past Jeshua and the soldiers holding him and speak to Eleazar, who nodded vigorously. Annas then spoke to the Council members behind Eleazar. Eleazar meanwhile waved to catch Pilate's attention.

'Prefect!' Eleazar shouted to him. 'We wish you to release Barabbas.'

With that the supporters to whom Annas had spoken started to shout 'Barabbas! Release Barabbas!' Others in the crowd quickly took up the chant. Then Jeshua's supporters caught on and chanted in reply: 'Jeshua! Release Jeshua'. Pilate scratched his brow in exasperation. Maximus moved towards him and spoke into his ear, both to maintain privacy and to be heard above the noise.

'Prefect, this will boil over very soon and people will

die,' said the Centurion urgently. Pilate nodded, noticing that some auxiliaries were glancing worriedly in his direction. They were beginning to doubt that they could maintain control.

'All the troops in the Palace are deployed,' said Maximus. 'You have to resolve this now, Sir, so we can clear the streets.' As Maximus stepped away Pilate looked at the crowds in front of him. Which half of the city should he upset?

'Jeshua of Nazareth,' Pilate called over the noise. Jeshua looked straight back at him through his one eye that had not closed due to the earlier beatings. 'These men are accusing you of capital offences. You know that I have the authority to sentence you to death. What do you say for yourself?' Through the noise Jeshua looked calmly at him and said nothing. Pilate shivered to see the mix of defiance and serenity in that stare. He had seen it before from Jeshua earlier that morning. He had seen it years earlier in the faces of those who had offered their necks to his own soldiers' swords, preferring to be killed rather than to abandon God.

In years to come he would look back and recall this as the moment when he realised, with clarity, that Jeshua was going to die. This was the moment Pilate realised that, since Jeshua was not trying to save himself, neither could he. Eleazar, the experienced trial lawyer, was watching for that moment too. As that realisation struck Pilate, Eleazar caught his eye and called out:

'If you don't find him guilty you are no friend of Caesar[44].'

Pilate and Eleazar held each other's gaze for a second. Shouts of 'Jeshua' and 'Barabbas' echoed around the small square. Then Pilate looked again at Jeshua and felt that he could see a challenge in the rabbi's eyes: are you going to risk the wrath of your Emperor and live at peace with yourself? Or are you going to do the expedient thing and live a quiet life? What is it to be, Pontius Pilate? Peace or quiet?

Pilate waved at Maximus, who stepped quickly back to his side. As Pilate looked straight into Joseph's eyes he knew he had lost. Eleazar's heart leaped in joy at Pilate's final words, not least at the likely impact on his future earnings.

'High Priest. I am innocent of this man's blood.[45] Centurion, arrange for Barabbas to be released to the High Priest. Jeshua of Nazareth is to be flogged and then crucified for sedition.'

CHAPTER 47

Golgotha, the crucifixion site, Friday mid-morning

When the trial was over, Jeshua and the two brigands captured with Barabbas were scourged by the soldiers, then led out to be crucified. Pilate's troops had relished another opportunity to be as cruel as possible to rebels. The flesh on Jeshua's back was badly shredded from the metal and bone studs set into the leather lashes of the scourges. As the duty centurion, Maximus followed the party through the streets and he saw the horror on the faces of the crowd at the extent of his injuries. To add further injury and insult, his soldiers had platted a crown from thorns and had pushed it onto his head[46]. The crowd dared do nothing but watch and, in some cases, weep.

Despite his wounds Jeshua had continued to command events. As the women wept he had told them to cry for themselves. He followed that with a terrifying prophecy, uttered as his blood dripped from him: 'Soon you will say "A blessing on the barren, a blessing on the wombs that never gave birth and a blessing on the breasts that never nursed children." If they do this to the green wood, imagine what they'll do to the dry.' In a world where children were themselves a blessing, not least because without children you might have no care in old age, that was an ominous blessing indeed.

One of the soldiers walking ahead carried a notice-board a couple of feet square, on which was written, in Greek, Aramaic and Latin, 'Jeshua of Nazareth, King of the Jews'[47]. It was to be nailed above Jeshua. Maximus could see the humour in Pilate's choice of words. He may have been outmanoeuvred into finding him guilty of an obvious *meiestas* charge but Pilate clearly intended to annoy the priests as best he could in return. Sure enough, as the execution party had set off, he had seen the priests arguing with Pilate's officials about it. Well, you wanted us to execute him for claiming to be king, Maximus thought, as he followed the soldiers taking the condemned men to their deaths.

The execution site chosen for that day was named Golgotha, after a rocky outcrop nearby which appeared like the scalp and eye-sockets of a human skull. It was just outside Jerusalem's walls and alongside a busy road, as was normal for such executions. This would maximise the number of locals who would see the penalty meted out to any who challenged Rome's authority. There is no point in rebelling against us, the degradation of crucifixion proclaimed to Rome's subject peoples.

It also meant that there had to be enough guards to ensure no one interfered with the executions. Any friends and family of the dying were always watched and it was not unknown for any suspected as fellow seditionists, or potential rescuers, to be summarily crucified alongside their loved ones.

Putting the men on their crosses was the same horrifyingly grisly event that it always was, in Maximus' experience. Jeshua was calm and dignified as he was stripped naked and surprisingly quiet as he was forced to lie on the cross and the spikes were hammered through his limbs.

211

Not so the two brigands. The first one pleaded for mercy through tears of terror. He cried like small child as his limbs were nailed to the wood and he gave an ear-splitting shriek as the cross was lifted vertically, his weight came onto the spikes and his flesh tore until he was supported on the bones of his limbs.

The second man had watched with horror as Jeshua and the other brigand were hung and, as what was left of his clothes were stripped off him, he kneed one of the soldiers holding him in the groin, then lunged for freedom. A second soldier tried to restrain him but the blood from his scourging wounds made the man's skin slippery and he wriggled out of the grasp. As shouts of excitement and encouragement went up from the bystanders he dashed for the road. He made it three paces before two more soldiers blocked his path and wrestled him to the floor. More soldiers joined in and as he fought for his freedom he was punched and kicked into some degree of submission before being carried, shouting and struggling, back to the waiting cross. The fight continued as, limb by limb, he was nailed onto the cross, the shouted curses increasingly mixed with screams of pain.

The second of the brigands shouted defiantly at the soldiers even when the cross was in place. At one point he abused Jeshua, shouting at him that if he was *messiah* why didn't he get them all down from the crosses. It was the same abusive taunt also being hurled at Jeshua by some in the crowd who, Maximus noticed, had been at the trial earlier that morning. At that point his less rebellious companion found enough courage within himself to tell him to shut up, pointing out that Jeshua was innocent while they were only getting the penalty for their crime. Jeshua had obviously appreciated the intervention and, between the effort required to breathe and withstand the unending pain himself, had offered him some words which, although Maximus couldn't hear them, clearly consoled the brigand[48].

By noon, the men were crucified and the guards were set to prevent rescue. The troops had divided up the men's clothes[49], their last possessions on earth as far as the authorities were aware, and they were left naked to die, a last extra humiliation. Jeshua had been wearing a single piece shirt, for which the soldiers had played dice and which had provided them with a few minutes of excitement. Now the boredom would set in. There was nothing left for the soldiers to do but to wait for death to come.

The dying men could allow their weight to be supported on the spikes through their ankles, which was excruciatingly painful but they could still breathe. Or they could hang on their arms, perhaps a little less painful, but breathing increasingly became more difficult. There would now follow a cycle of supporting their weight alternately by arms, then legs, as their strength faded. Eventually they would suffocate.

Some executioners thoughtfully placed a bar on the cross for the victim to stand on, which meant the death was delayed and the pain lengthened. Today though, speed was the priority. Tonight the Hebrew Sabbath started so all three were to be dead by sunset. A large mallet with a handle a yard long had been brought by the troops; it would be used to break their legs an hour or so before sunset. Then unsupported by the lower spike they would suffocate in time.

Maximus had overseen the process but his men had known what they were doing and needed no guidance from him. Instead he had reflected on the contrast between the two dying for rebellion and Jeshua, who had submitted to his fate knowing he was innocent. Was that a clue to his enigmatic comment on the fate of dry and green wood, one easy to burn, the other very difficult?

He knew Jeshua had threatened a judgement of destruction on Jerusalem, and the Jewish nation with it, if they refused to follow the path he, Jeshua, had laid out for them as God's path. Did Jeshua see the Romans as the means of God's judgement, he wondered? He wasn't the first Jew to suggest that violence against Rome would only result in destruction. Jeshua saw himself as the "green wood" and crucifixion had happened to a man preaching repentance and reconciliation. So what fire would consume the "dry wood": the hotheads who saw violence as a route to peace and freedom?

Even more enigmatic was a prayer Jeshua uttered as he struggled to breath amidst his pain. Maximus heard that: "Forgive them, Father, They don't know what they're doing," he had said. Was "Father" the God whose kingdom he said he was creating, this kingdom not of this world?

From all he had seen and heard this was a strange kingdom. Jeshua offered the peace of his kingdom to all the wrong people and upset those who might have thought of themselves as obvious members. Instead of threatening Romans, like him, with judgement, as the Jews might have expected, he warned God would judge the Jews and, not least, their leaders. He hung now, proclaimed as King of the Jews, but only by his Roman executioners and as an explanation for his death.

Perhaps strangest of all, Jeshua didn't curse his enemies that killed him, as rebels like the Maccabees had in the past. Maximus would have expected that of Barabbas but for his last-minute exchange of fate. Instead, Jeshua had prayed that this God would forgive them since they didn't know what they were doing: the priests who gave him to us, the Prefect who sentenced him, my men who are torturing him to death. Perhaps even myself, thought Maximus. So what am I doing that I don't know?

Two groups of ten men had been assigned to the guard. One group would now be active around the crosses, the other could relax but be on site to provide extra muscle if there was trouble. Satisfied that his troops were sufficient and properly deployed, Maximus had seen no point in staying at the site himself as he had plenty of other work to do. The condemned weren't going anywhere and his men were perfectly capable of managing any onlookers. A few civilians shouted insults at Jeshua but even they tended to keep moving. In fact, apart from a few of Jeshua's followers, most passing by did so hurriedly. They knew and feared the risks of being associated with the dying, a fear Maximus knew his men would reinforce at every opportunity, if only to relieve boredom.

All bar one of those at the foot of Jeshua's cross were women. Did that surprise Maximus? He knew the number of women who followed Jeshua had often caused much comment among the respectable. As he started back to the Antonia Fortress he thought he recognised one of the faces from the party that Jeshua had led around the Temple earlier that week. So where were the other male followers? Or had Jeshua just picked a bunch of cowards?

As for the other two, no one was there for them. What had led them into Barabbas' band, he wondered? Were there wives and children somewhere waiting for husbands who will now never come home? Sad, he thought, to die all alone.

As he had been walking through the Damascus Gate the light had started to fail. By the time he had got back to the Antonia Fortress it was dark[50]. Eclipses were common and this one would doubtless be recorded as one of many such occurrences. It would keep the soothsayers and diviners gainfully employed for months. The gullible were always willing to pay for interpretations of "omens". On the other hand, the wisest Roman knew that many bad things happened when eclipses occurred. There had been an eclipse when the Emperor Augustus died twenty or so years earlier. Legend told that Romulus himself, the founder of Rome, had died during an eclipse. At the back of his Roman mind, Maximus was always willing to wonder whether the gods might indeed be angry about something.

He couldn't work in the dark, so took a lamp-lit lunch with some of the other officers of the garrison while the light returned. He then managed an hour or so in the office after that. In the middle of the afternoon, he returned to the site. It wouldn't be long before it would be time to break legs so the crucified died before sunset at the twelfth hour. He arrived, in fact, in time for the most unusual end to an execution he had ever seen.

CHAPTER 48

Golgotha, Friday mid-afternoon

Maximus had been chatting to his troops for a few minutes when they heard Jeshua cry out in his pain[51]: *'Eloi, Eloi, lema sabachthani?'*

The soldiers looked up at Jeshua hanging above them, almost as if they had forgotten he was there. Aramaic speakers all, some sniggered and chuckled as they looked at each other. The cry caused a more emotional response amongst the women. An older woman, who Maximus guessed might be Jeshua's mother, burst into tears and ran to hug the cross, reaching out gently to touch his feet. Just as she did so two guards grabbed her and bundled her away. Hoping to avoid a confrontation two younger women also took hold of her and firmly led her away, comforting her as they did. A third reassured the soldiers that she was no threat. A soldier shouted at Jeshua to shut up and backed up the demand by throwing a stone, which hit Jeshua on the chest. There was a round of applause at the throw.

Two merchants, leading a loaded donkey, heard the cry and stopped for a moment to look at the crucified men. 'Listen!' said one to his friend and they both studied Jeshua intently. 'Isn't he calling for Elijah?'

'What did he say?' Maximus asked them in Aramaic,

pointing up at Jeshua. The two Judeans looked at him, then at each other and back to Maximus.

'Roughly speaking, he's asking God why he's been forsaken,' one replied.

'Or he might be trying to summon Elijah. One of our prophets,' said the other, assuming Maximus knew nothing of Hebrew history. 'He's probably thirsty too. Can I give him a drink?' he asked Maximus. 'Then let's see if Elijah comes to save him,' he suggested excitedly to his friend. The other man smiled at the thought.

'Carry on,' said Maximus and nodded to the decanus in charge of the site. The man pulled a sponge from a pack on the donkey, filled it with wine from a flask, then put it on one of the poles that the troops had used to push the cross up into the vertical. He held it to Jeshua's lips. Jeshua took a drink but a hiss as he took a breath, and then the grimace on his face afterwards, suggested it was probably sour and that he might now regret having done so. Some also dripped from the sponge into wounds around his neck and shoulders and would have stung enormously. Maximus heard Jeshua groan again, then say to himself. 'It is finished.' Then Jeshua became still and was silent.

The soldiers lost interest and started chatting among themselves. Maximus and the decanus watched for a few more moments and then Jeshua cried out again in a loud voice. Any words were unintelligible but, as if he had decided to die at that moment, he breathed out deeply and was still. Maximus and his subordinate looked at each other and back at Jeshua's limp body.

'Do you think he's dead, Sir?' asked the decanus. Before Maximus could answer though, the ground shook[52] and kept shaking. Though the tremors were not particularly violent, the soldiers braced themselves against a nearby rock. The donkey backed away from his masters in panic and there was alarm amongst the troops. The donkey's owners struggled to control him. He bucked and one of them cried in pain as a hoof stamped on his foot. Despite their alarm at the tremors, some of the soldiers laughed as the man hopped about, one foot in his hands, cursing loudly. Then as quickly as they started the tremors ceased. There was a distant crash, which sounded like falling masonry, equally distant shouts of alarm, then stillness and quiet.

The pain in the donkey owner's foot also subsided, albeit more slowly. He came back to where the donkey stood next to the other man and kicked the beast hard on its back leg. The animal brayed in protest and moved, obviously attempting to get out of range of any further retribution. As it happened, the one kick had satisfied the man's anger.

Maximus and the decanus checked the crosses. The other two men were clearly still alive. Maximus looked at the sun and decided that there was only a couple of hours of daylight remaining. He told the decanus that he could break their legs. The soldiers had been waiting for that and got up excitedly, one running to the mallet. In whiling away the hours they had played dice to select the order in they would get to swing blows. As the winner stepped up to the crosses there was a hail of good-natured advice about where to aim the mallet. The two victims suddenly realised what was about to happen to them and both started screaming. One begged for someone to finish him off with a spear first but the soldiers laughed and told him they would break his legs first. The women looked up with horror, then either covered their eyes with their headdresses, or looked away, hands over their mouths.

Meanwhile Maximus and the decanus were looking up at Jeshua hanging lifelessly from his cross.

'Looks like he's dead,' ventured the decanus. 'What do you think, Sir?'

'Does, doesn't it?' agreed Maximus. 'We can't …' a piercing scream cut off his words and he paused looking up to the man on the next cross. There was a round of applause as the lucky soldier who had swung the blow took a bow from his colleagues and handed the mallet over to the soldier who had obviously come second in the leg-breaking game. The only man among Jeshua's followers turned away and threw up.

Maximus waited while the next man swung the mallet at the man's other shin, connecting midway between the ankle and the knee. It snapped with a slight crunch and this was followed instantly by another piercing scream, which kept on coming between breaths. He struggled, trying in vain to find any position that eased any of the different sources of pain. As he struggled against the spikes he drove himself into panic. His screams became howls. Any modesty that had survived being hung naked in public failed at this point and his bowels opened, urine and excrement flowing in spurts down his legs. The soldier with the mallet wasn't quite quick enough to leave and there were jeers of derision from his fellows as he was caught in the filth. A third soldier wrested the mallet from him and tried to wipe it on the other's clothing but failed. Laughing, he advanced to the second victim who babbled loudly at his approach.

'I was about to say,' continued Maximus, over the screaming and cheering, 'that we need to make sure he's dead. Get someone to spear him in the chest. Then, either way, he'll definitely be dead.'

Breaking the second man's legs took longer than the first. The third man was younger and at the crucial moment his nerve failed him. He swung without the conviction of his older colleagues. The mallet hit the target but without enough momentum. The man screamed in pain but his leg didn't break. The soldiers jeered at the youngster who accepted the criticism with an embarrassed wave, and handed the mallet to another, older and more grizzled, soldier. His blow, and that of the next man were surer. Once the second man's legs had been broken the decanus spoke to another soldier, apparently the next winner of the mallet-swinging prize. He jogged forward enthusiastically with a spear. There was also a ripple of disappointment though; if Jeshua was already dead, the leg-breaking was over.

Maximus and the decanus looked up at Jeshua's body and nodded to the man, who placed the point of his spear under Jeshua's ribs. The *pilum* was constructed from a metal shaft and point protruding a couple of feet from a wider wooden shaft. The soldier heaved the tip into Jeshua's lungs and pushed it up through his chest until the wider part of the wooden shaft of the spear was stopped by the flesh. The body made no reaction. The soldier twisted the weapon and pulled it back with all the weight he could apply. The point came out with a squelching sound followed by a steady flow of blood and water[53]. There was no pulsing emission, so Jeshua's heart had stopped. The three of them looked at each other and agreed that he was clearly dead.

CHAPTER 49

Maximus glanced at the other two men. Their screams were subsiding as they focussed on the mechanics of breathing. The beatings, the hours of pain, the shock and the blood loss had already exhausted them so as they rasped for breath. Maximus knew that they would be dead soon. He found a spot where he could wait comfortably and watch for the end. Then he could report the deaths and see his men back to barracks. Like all soldiers, he was used to waiting patiently for things to happen.

As the minutes passed, he reflected on events: you'd get long odds against either an earthquake or an eclipse on any given day. Even longer against both on the same day. He looked again at Jeshua's body and wondered. Was there something significant about this rabbi after all?

He knew there were natural explanations for earthquakes. Maximus could remember explaining to his troops before that eclipses do happen. Earthquakes were common in these parts. "It's just the earth farting", he remembered someone saying, to general merriment at the time. Maximus though, like all Romans, knew there were forces beyond nature too. Privately he wasn't sure what those forces were or how they and the gods related to the world he knew. Beyond the material world he knew, though, he could feel another to which it was somehow connected. Everything suggested this man was clearly

222

special in some way. Had nature or the gods recognised something too? Had the earth convulsed as nature watched a god die?

Jeshua's people left one by one. Maximus admired the loyalty with which the women, and that one man, had risked staying with him. Most of all he had been impressed at how well Jeshua died, something much admired by Romans and respected even in their enemies. He smiled admiringly at the corpse. We took everything he had from him, yet Jeshua had faced his death with dignity and wouldn't let us choose when he died. Most amazingly Maximus thought, he was innocent but still forgave those who executed him. Pilate would want to know that Jeshua had died well. He wondered idly if anyone might write a biography of Jeshua's life. He'd only briefly met him but Maximus decided he was a man whose life was probably worth copying.

As the sun sank into the western sky, the longest lasting of the two men crucified with Jeshua could breathe no more. There were a final few convulsions, as he found he could no longer draw breath and the panic of suffocation took him. His strength was almost gone and his brain, starved of oxygen, shut down. As he twitched ever less, the soldiers began to gather their kit, knowing they would soon be off duty. Finally he too was still.

After a few more minutes, Maximus checked the bodies and, satisfied all three were dead, was happy to leave the bodies for the locals. As his men marched away, he saw a horseman riding fast towards them. Maximus guessed the rider had business with him. Bit late for a reprieve, he thought, glancing up at the bodies motionless on their crosses.

'Centurion!' called the rider. 'The Prefect needs you as soon as possible in the Herodian Palace. I'm to give you this horse. He needs to know about Jeshua of Nazareth.'

CHAPTER 50

The Palace of Herod, Friday afternoon

Maximus' horse clattered, a little wildly, to a halt in the square outside the front of Pilate's Palace. As an infantryman he shared the Roman army's widespread disdain of horses. When he rode it was for necessity rather than pleasure and he distrusted unfamiliar animals. A groom ran from the main doorway and took over the horse once Maximus had dismounted. The centurion strode through the main door, returning the salutes offered by the guards. As he made straight for Pilate's offices, he removed his sweat-soaked helmet, then rubbed his close-cropped hair with his hand. One of Pilate's secretaries was waiting for him and, taking the helmet, ushered him through a door into one of the anterooms to the Governor's office. Maximus was given a towel, invited to take a drink and assured that Pilate wouldn't keep him waiting. In fact the door of Pilate's office swung open before he finished pouring the drink. Pilate himself appeared.

'Centurion,' he said, 'I'd hoped that was your arrival I heard. Come straight in, please,' Pilate noted both the drink and the sweat and smiled faintly, 'and bring the drink through.'

Maximus followed the Governor into his office,

managing to empty the glass by the time he reached the other side of the anteroom, then neatly passing the empty to a slave who happened to be standing just inside the door to Pilate's office a few feet away.

'Jeshua. What news?' asked Pilate.

'Jeshua of Nazareth, Sir?'

'He's the only Jeshua I know of, Centurion,' Pilate snapped slightly, 'unless there's another sent by the gods to spoil the rest of my day the way he spoiled the start of it.'

Maximus smiled faintly. 'He's the only one I know of too. And he is dead, Sir.'

Pilates eyes narrowed. 'Are you sure?'

'I'm certain, Sir. We ran him through the chest with a spear. I checked his body myself. He didn't even wait for us to break his legs. Having decided this morning that he would have us execute him, he then decided to die when he was ready, not when we let him go.' Pilate frowned at this and Maximus went on. 'I wondered about the darkness, then that earthquake happened almost the minute he went. Didn't he say his kingdom wasn't of this world? If his kingdom really is beyond this world, it seems it's got an impressive reach.'

'Are you saying he was a god himself, Centurion?' asked Pilate suspiciously.

'I wouldn't presume to know about gods, Sir.'

'Nor me,' muttered Pilate darkly then added. 'So he died well then?'

'He certainly died as memorably as it seems he lived.'

'That doesn't surprise me,' Pilate looked as though he was about to say something else but changed his mind. At that moment there was a knock on the doors on the other side of the office.

'Come in!' called Pilate.

The door swung open and an elderly Hebrew was

shown in. From his clothes the man was clearly a wealthy businessman. He bowed politely towards Pilate. A Roman scribe had come in with him carrying a small scroll.

'Ah, Joseph, come in. Jeshua is dead. You may take the body.[54]'

Pilate took the scroll from the scribe, glanced at the contents and then signed and sealed it. He gave it to Joseph and turned to Maximus.

'Centurion, This is Joseph, of Arimathea, a friend of Jeshua's family. He has a tomb in a garden near the execution site. Please provide him with an escort to the site to ensure he can remove Jeshua's body for burial. From what you've just said he doesn't deserve to be tossed into Gehenna with the rest of the rubbish.'

While they had waited for Maximus to arrive, Joseph had told Pilate that Jeshua had often used the image of the bonfires that seemed to be permanently smouldering in Gehenna, Jerusalem's rubbish dump in the Hinnon Valley, as an image of judgement. Pilate smiled at the irony that Jeshua's body had nearly ended up there itself.

Joseph bowed again to Pilate and left through the door he had entered by. Maximus saluted and followed him. Pilate, ignoring the slave who was still standing quietly by the door through which Maximus had entered, filled a cup with water from a jug on a small table, then stretched out on a couch with a sigh and closed his eyes. A few moments later the door swung open to admit Claudia Procula.

'Have you finished for the day, then? Any news? I saw the Centurion leaving with Joseph of Arimathea.'

Pilate looked at his wife but otherwise lay still on the couch. 'Jeshua is dead and I've asked Maximus to release the body. Joseph wants to bury him.'

'I'm glad its over. I hope killing an innocent man won't come back to haunt us.'

'Not as much as Tiberius would haunt us if he heard that I am soft on seditionists and rebels.' Pilate pointed out.

'You're probably right,' she nodded. 'So have you finished for the day? We're at a dinner tonight, aren't we?'

Pilate brightened immediately and smiled. 'Oh yes! I'd forgotten. Good! Just what we need to put this business behind us and move on. Come on, I need a bath.'

PART SIX

ANNO DOMINUS

CHAPTER 51

Caesarea Maritima, Pilate's Palace, a Sunday evening, late June

Pilate lay on his favourite couch on his terrace in Caesarea Maritima, enjoying the sea view, the mid-summer sunset and the breeze on his cheek. He sipped some wine as the warmth of the sun and the light wind helped him to relax. His eyes closed as the stresses of the day slipped gently from his consciousness. He vaguely heard a swish of fabric as the curtains dividing the balcony from the chamber behind moved. Soft footfalls were followed moments later by an embarrassed cough. Pilate opened his eyes to see Festus Maximus stood in front of the curtains.

'Centurion! Good to see you out of uniform. Welcome to the coast! Was the journey from Jerusalem good?'

'Fast and uneventful, thank you, Prefect. I even got here early enough this afternoon for a bath.'

'Good, it'll be a good dinner tonight too. As I promised in my letter, I have invited some people who might help you retire well after your illustrious career. Those of us who've served together should stick together, I think. I hope a few introductions might help anyway. Have a drink?' Pilate waved vaguely in the direction of a slave standing beside a table set with food and drinks.

'I am very grateful for your interest, Prefect. I can't

231

imagine anything that will ever give me the satisfaction that the Army has. I'm always happy to listen to advice.' Maximus nodded at the slave who was already poised to pour him a glass. He took some meat from a plate as the wine was poured and some olives as he accepted the cup.

'Take a seat,' said Pilate. 'This view is one of the bonuses of this job. Beautiful, don't you think?'

'I think I would have my headquarters here too, given the choice, Sir,' Maximus chuckled as he sat, slightly formally, on one of the other couches.

'Avé,' Pilate laughed as he raised his glass in a toast.

'Your health, Prefect!' Maximus responded and they drank, savouring the wine.

'I gather nothing much is happening in Jerusalem?' said Pilate, lying back on his couch.

'If you mean the uprising, I think we've seen the last of the zealots, for now at least, Sir. The ringleaders are dead or fled into exile. We've tidied up lots of weapons. I think we're back to business as usual.'

'Barabbas?'

'No sign of him,' Maximus replied with a shake of the head. 'We think he left the country. If he's any sense he's headed east to India or somewhere equally out of reach. He knows he's a dead man if we get him again.'

'Pity we had to let him go. He was quite a catch for you. It was you who caught him, wasn't it?'

'That's right, Sir,' Maximus nodded and smiled that Pilate still remembered that kind of detail.

'Militarily it was a poor swap, letting him loose and hanging that poor rabbi instead. I'm sorry about that.'

'In the circumstances what else could we have done?'

'The priests outmanoeuvred me.'

'I wouldn't put it quite like that, Sir,' Maximus replied, with no trace of irony.

'I would,' Pilate frowned and glanced at Maximus, 'but I'm grateful that you understand the position I was in. It was hardly the best outcome though. I couldn't really see Jeshua leading an uprising. Did you know my wife went to see him quite a few times? She was very sad that we had to crucify him.'

'The Emperor would not have been pleased if we'd let him go, though,' pointed out Maximus.

'Well absolutely. The first duty of a government is security and the protection of the citizens, isn't it? We can't let radicals go free just because they haven't got round to committing crimes yet, can we?'

'No, certainly not,' agreed Maximus, then added, 'by the way, have you heard his followers are claiming Jeshua rose from the dead?' Maximus chuckled. 'A few days after he was buried.'

'What?' Pilate turned onto his side and looked at Maximus. 'Hah! I'll bet that's wound up the High Priest,' he laughed, 'Caiaphas must be livid! Come to think of it, wasn't there a story that he brought someone back to life just before he was executed?'

'Yes, sir. Caiaphas put that one down to either trickery or sorcery and I think he's taking the same view of Jeshua's resurrection.'

'Hold on.' Pilate's eyes narrowed. 'You said "resurrection". Do you actually mean coming back to life *in this world as a body*?' Pilate emphasised the words and the disbelief grew in his tone. 'Not reincarnated? Not back in spirit? Not just that they've seen his ghost? They're claiming his body has actually come alive again?'

'Yes, resurrection. Precisely that,' nodded Maximus. 'The Temple people just say that his disciples stole the body from the tomb of course. Meanwhile there are thousands of people in Jerusalem now worshipping 'the Risen Lord'. No doubt the story is spreading to the other Hebrew communities around the Empire too.'

'The Risen Lord! That's almost sedition. Caesar is Lord. Are they comparing Jeshua to the Emperor? Politically, that really could be taken as a challenge to the authority of Rome,' said Pilate. 'You confirmed Jeshua was actually dead, didn't you?'

'Yes, and the Temple Guard Captain has been derisory about my judgement too.' Maximus grinned as he took another sip of wine. 'But Jeshua was definitely dead before he was taken off the cross. As far as I'm concerned he still is.'

'Haven't they found the body then? The Temple people must have torn Jerusalem apart looking.'

'They did and they still haven't,' Maximus nodded. 'Not that there'll be much left of it by now. The Temple are just trying to dismiss the whole issue.'

'I'll bet,' laughed Pilate.

'I'm surprised the disciples came back and stole his body though,' added Maximus thoughtfully. 'By the time we'd finished they had all deserted him. He's not the first "anointed one" we've executed either. No one claimed they'd resurrected.'

'How intriguing,' mused Pilate. 'Are we taking any further action?'

'Because someone reports a dead person alive again?' Maximus asked, looking at Pilate and raised his eyebrows. Pilate started to laugh.

'Exactly, Sir,' Maximus smiled too. 'I'm not about to risk my pension turning out the guard to look for someone whom I personally saw die, am I? Anyway, what would I tell the men they're looking for?'

'A rather pale man, dressed in a burial shroud?' asked Pilate. Then he laughed imagining the briefing to the troops. 'Distinguishing features: nail holes in his ankles and wrists. Didn't you have to kill him before a Sabbath?' Pilate paused. 'With two broken legs. No, no. He died before you needed to break his legs, didn't he? Didn't you run him through with a spear or something?'

'That's right, Sir.' Maximus was also laughing at the thought of a briefing for a search for a live corpse. He took another swig of wine.

'Look out for a large spear wound to the chest, men!' Pilate laughed, then lowered his voice and added in dramatic tones, 'and keep your noses peeled for a whiff of decay.' Both men laughed helplessly, Pilate putting his glass on a nearby table to avoid spilling it. Both slaves attending them worked hard to keep their faces straight too.

'So am I going to risk a charge of insanity?' asked Maximus, as the their laughter subsided. 'There's no reason for us to get involved. It'll blow over.' He took another sip of his drink.

'Quite,' nodded Pilate, laughing once more as he relaxed back onto his couch. 'The Mystery of the Disappearing Holyman,' Pilate mused for a few moments, then added: 'You know, it might make a good play.'

'Do you have a theatrical side?' asked Maximus.

'Oh, I like a bit of a drama, yes,' replied Pilate. 'How do Jeshua's disciples say he came back to life, then?'

'Funnily enough, when you talk to them they seem just as surprised as everyone else. Apparently some of Jeshua's women went to the tomb after the Sabbath with all the spices so they could carry on with the first stage of the burial process[55]. They were shocked to find the tomb empty, so they were clearly expecting him still to be dead.'

'Well that's no good as a story!' said Pilate scornfully. 'I don't think anyone's actually written about someone who came back from the dead into this world. But if someone did, the women finding the body wrecks the story before you start.'

'Sorry, Sir? Why?' asked Maximus. Pilate turned and looked at him.

'Well the first question anyone will ask is: "Who saw him alive?" Pilate explained. 'And the answer is "the women"? Who is going to believe women?' Pilate took a swig from his glass. 'His disciples will have to do much better than that.' Pilate lay back on the couch. 'Did Jeshua have a wife then?'

'No, unusually for a Jew his age,' replied Maximus. 'Lots of women followed him though.'

'So how did the women at the tomb know it was him?' asked Pilate.

'He's unmistakable, apparently. He seems to have turned up all over the place since too. That chap from Arimathea you gave his body to? He says he's seen him.'

'Joseph? You're joking! He's a friend of Nicodemus. He doesn't believe this, surely?'

'There's a rumour Nicodemus believes it too. Joseph says he was with some of Jeshua's supporters in a house in Jerusalem when Jeshua appeared[56]. There wasn't any knock at the door or anything. He just appeared.'

'So he was a ghost then,' said Pilate.

'Well, no,' Maximus shook his head. 'That's the mystery.'

'Sounds like a ghost to me,' observed Pilate, 'if he walks through walls.'

'Well that's what the disciples thought at first too. Joseph said they were terrified. Jeshua had quite a bit of trouble convincing them he wasn't a ghost.'

'And you can see why, can't you?' laughed Pilate. 'Imagine if someone that we both knew was dead just appeared through those curtains with a cheery "Hello".'

Maximus glanced towards the back of the balcony and nodded. The slave by the curtains, who had been listening avidly, glanced nervously at the curtain to reassure himself that there was no such presence. 'We'd both be terrified too,' mused Pilate. 'Did he convince them he wasn't a ghost then?'

'Joseph wasn't sure. Jeshua apparently ate some food. Do ghosts do that?' asked Maximus.

'No idea,' Pilate shrugged his shoulders. 'I've never met one. So Joseph believes in this resurrection then?'

'Yes. Which is strange, isn't it? He's no fool.'

'I definitely wouldn't put Joseph among the fanciful of this world,' agreed Pilate.

'In fact he was almost apologetic about it,' Maximus continued. 'He told me: "We all know dead people don't come back to life, but that's what we saw."'

'Am I surprised they weren't expecting it then?' said Pilate. 'When we kill people, they generally stay dead.'

Pilate sipped his wine again then something else struck him.

'Centurion, is this "anointed one" supposed to come back from the dead?'

'Most Jews believe that all righteous people will come back from the dead,' replied Maximus, 'but only at the end of time. I think most Jews expect the "anointed one" to clear pagans like us out of the Hebrew lands, not die on a cross. At the moment most Hebrews think that the fact that we killed him proves he isn't *messiah*. I think there's also a curse against anyone hung on a cross too. That's probably why his disciples gave up on him.'

'So the idea of a bodily resurrection, like this, is genuinely new, even to the Jews? As a story, I mean? I can't think of a Roman or Greek writing about it. I've heard about ghosts or becoming a star in the heavens. Or a god like

Caesar if you are good enough. Or being reincarnated. But everyone knows no one comes back to *this* world a second time, don't they?'

'Of course not,' agreed Maximus, 'and I don't know of anyone who tells stories about it either.' Whenever he had spoken to Jeshua's disciples since he died he'd increasingly wished he'd had a chance to meet the man while he'd been alive. This resurrection rumour now added one more to the questions that Maximus would already want to ask him. What makes hundreds of sensible people suddenly believe something happened that they all still say cannot happen?

'Here's a thought, Prefect,' said Maximus, 'Joseph pointed out that if their single and universal God wanted to provide everyone in the world with a sign that no power on earth could produce, something that could only come from God, raising a dead person from the grave would be pretty unmistakeable, wouldn't it?'

'Unmistakable?' Pilate asked. He took another sip of wine, relaxed and closed his eyes as he pondered that thought. As he felt the evening breeze on his face he smiled to himself at the thought of Caiaphas and Annas trying to find a more convincing natural explanation.

Crucifixion followed by bodily resurrection? If no one's thought of it before it would make a great mystery play, he mused. If Jeshua's disciples have made up the story they have it totally wrong though. They'll need reliable men as witnesses. No one will ever believe them if they keep saying the women found the tomb empty.

EPILOGUE

What does reading the Bible and Shakespeare have in common? One answer is that unless you understand the culture, language and writing conventions of their times they can be hard to follow, not least because its harder to get the jokes. In writing *The Blood of Innocents* I have tried to find a way of describing the events of the first Easter so that those more familiar with 21st century writing can still sense why that Passover, some 2,000 years ago, has had such lasting significance. Many news stories today are driven by the same conflicts and ideas that led Jeshua, son of Joseph, to be executed on the first Good Friday.

I have not sought to tell, directly, the story that is told in the four gospels, the biographies of Jesus in the New Testament and, to various extents, in the works of other writers of that time. This is not another gospel and, though I like to think the Holy Spirit guided its creation, it is not in any way to be compared with the canonical gospels. It is just my attempt, based on what we know did, or probably, happened, to tell a story that describes what drove the events around the death and resurrection of Jesus.

Those two events really did take place, in my belief, and had all the significance that Jesus' followers, including many Jews, have always said they had. Where the Bible's gospel writers chose not to specify detail I have guessed at the detail that led them to write what they wrote. When the gospel writers say, for example, that there were plots against Jesus, I have tried to imagine who the plotters may have been and what they thought they were seeing. This, I hope, gives some clues, through both the real and invented characters, about why they made the decisions they actually made.

I discovered that putting myself in their shoes showed me how easy it would have been for me to have made the same decisions as they did. The wrong decisions but maybe for the right reasons.

I am grateful to many people for reading and commenting on various drafts and their comments helped me refine the manuscript. Some were asked because of their theological and literary training. Others were asked because they have none and gave insights from different gifts and perspectives. As author the final responsibility for the work is mine. As I now commit this to print I am most conscious of my responsibility to the real subject of this story, Jesus himself. Inevitably my portrayal of him was forged in my walk with Jesus in my own life. Where the best I can do isn't good enough I can only remind myself that faith in Jesus offers forgiveness of weakness and even deliberate fault. No religion born of humanity can offer such grace. God's redemption at Christ's expense.

For those who wish to read about the life of Jesus for themselves I would recommend starting by reading the gospels, perhaps in the reverse order. I have listed below the points, in the gospels and some other texts, where the events that I have mentioned in my story are described.

C.S. Lewis once wrote *"Christianity, if false, is of no importance, and if true, of infinite importance. The only thing it cannot be is moderately important."* I believe that Jesus is the same.

NOTES

[1] Matthew 5:5
[2] Matthew 5:39
[3] Matthew 20:25
[4] I Kings 18:20-40
[5] Matthew 11:3; Luke 7:19
[6] Matthew 19:24; Mark 10:25; Luke 18:25
[7] John 11:17
[8] John 1:46
[9] Matthew 2:1
[10] Matthew 2:16
[11] Various, including Matthew 11:15, 13:9,13:43; Mark 4:9, 4:23; Luke 8:8, 14:35
[12] John 9:1-41
[13] Luke 7:2-10
[14] Luke 1:26-56
[15] From Isaiah 9
[16] Matthew 5
[17] Matthew 6:10
[18] Matthew 13:3-21; Mark 4:3-20; Luke 8:4-15
[19] Matthew 14:3-12
[20] Luke 7:18-35
[21] Luke 10:25-37
[22] Psalm 23
[23] Mark 11:11
[24] Matthew 5 esp. 41-43

[25] Mark 5:21-43

[26] Matthew 21:23; Mark 11:28; Luke 20:1

[27] Matthew 21:28-31; Mark 12:1-12

[28] Matthew 21:33-46; Mark 12:1-12; Luke 20: 9-19

[29] Matthew 22:23-33; Mark 12; 18-27; Luke 20:27-40

[30] Matthew 22:15-22: Mark 12:13-17; Luke 20:20-26

[31] 1 Maccabees 2:68

[32] Josephus, *Antiquities of the Jews*, Book 18, Chapter 1

[33] Psalm 96:7

[34] Psalm 32:1-11

[35] John 8:3-11

[36] Matthew 26:57-66; Mark 14:53-64; Luke 22:66-71; John 18:12-27

[37] Matthew 26:47-56; Mark 14:43-50; Luke 22:47-53; John 18:3-10

[38] Matthew 26:63-64; Mark 14:61-63; Luke 22:67-70

[39] Matthew 26: 67-68; Mark 14:65; Luke 22:63

[40] Luke 23:2

[41] John 18:33

[42] Luke 23:6

[43] Matthew 27:15-23; Mark 15:8-14; Luke 23:18-23

[44] John 19:12

[45] Matthew 27:24

[46] Matthew 27:27-31; Mark 15:15-20

[47] Matthew 27: 37; Mark 15:25-26; Luke 23:37; John 19:19-22

[48] Luke 23: 39-43

[49] Matthew 27: 35; Mark 15:24; John 19:23-25

[50] Matthew 27:45; Mark 15:33; Luke 23:44

[51] Matthew 27:45-50; Mark 15:34; John 19:29

[52] Matthew 27:51

[53] John 19:34;

[54] Matthew 27:57-58; Mark 15:42-47; Luke 23:50-56; John 19:38-42

[55] Matthew 28: Mark 16; Luke 24; John 20 & 21

[56] Luke 24:36-49

Branch	Date
Sm	03/13